The Battle

Nancy Rue

PUBLISHING
Colorado Springs, Colorado

THE BATTLE
Copyright © 1997 by Nancy N. Rue
All rights reserved. International copyright secured.

Library of Congress Cataloging-in-Publication Data
Rue, Nancy N.
    The battle / Nancy Rue.
        p.   cm.—(Christian heritage series, the Williamsburg years ; 12)
    Summary: While the Revolutionary War rages all around him, twelve-year-old Thomas
fights his own internal battles involving anger, frustration, and lack of trust in God.

    ISBN 1-56179-542-9
    [1. Christian life—Fiction. 2. Anger—Fiction. 3. United States—History—Revolution,
1775-1783—Fiction.] I. Title. II. Series: Rue, Nancy N. Christian heritage series, ; bk. 12.
PZ7.R85515Bat   1997
[Fic]—dc20   97-2494
                                                                                                              CIP
                                                                                                              AC

Published by Focus on the Family Publishing,
Colorado Springs, Colorado 80995
Distributed in the U.S.A. and Canada by Word Books, Dallas, Texas

This author is represented by the literary agency of Alive Communications, 1465 Kelly
Johnson Blvd., Suite 320, Colorado Springs, CO 80920.

This is a work of fiction, an any resemblance between the characters in this book and real
persons is coincidental.

Editor: Keith Wall
Cover Design: Bradley Lind
Cover Illustration: Cheri Bladholm

Printed in the United States of America

97 98 99 00/10 9 8 7 6 5 4 3 2 1

*For Susie Shellenberger,
who knows what real freedom is
—and is always ready to share it.*

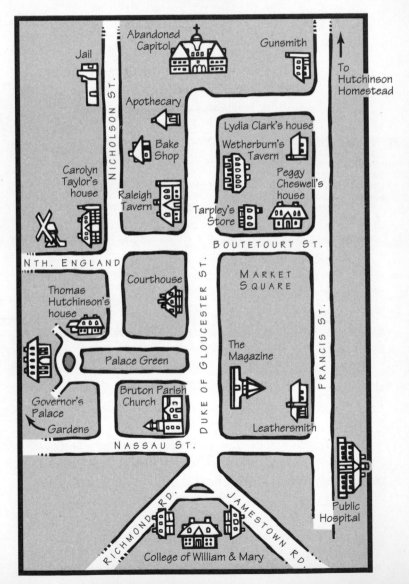

A Map of
Williamsburg
1780-81

Jail

Abandoned Capitol

Gunsmith

To Hutchinson Homestead

NICHOLSON ST.

Apothecary

Bake Shop

Lydia Clark's house

Wetherburn's Tavern

Carolyn Taylor's house

Raleigh Tavern

Peggy Cheswell's house

Tarpley's Store

NTH. ENGLAND

BOUTETOURT ST.

Courthouse

MARKET SQUARE

Thomas Hutchinson's house

DUKE OF GLOUCESTER ST.

FRANCIS ST.

Palace Green

The Magazine

Governor's Palace

Bruton Parish Church

Gardens

Leathersmith

NASSAU ST.

Public Hospital

RICHMOND RD.

JAMESTOWN RD.

College of William & Mary

Chapter One

"**T**om Hutchinson, if you sink my boat, so help me, I'll never speak to you again!"

Thomas Hutchinson grinned at Caroline Taylor, whose blonde brows were puckered fiercely at him above her round, brown eyes.

"You will too speak," Thomas said, giving her tiny leaf boat a shove down the stream with his stick. "I'd be hard put to try and stop you."

Caroline glared at him again as she leaned over the stream and plunged her arms in up to the elbow ruffles.

"Are you saying that I talk too much?" she said.

"Never," Thomas said quickly.

"I'm going to put this boat back into the water, and it's going to race yours," she said, tossing her straight, blonde hair over her shoulders. "And there will be no more cheating."

"Cheating!"

"Yes. Poking with sticks and other such nonsense."

"This kind of nonsense?" Thomas said. He poked the stick

1

playfully into her side. She scrambled up, petticoats flying.

"Give me that stick, Tom!" she cried. Thomas tossed the stick behind him and snatched both of her little wrists. She wriggled to get free, but he stood like a brick chimney, grinning down at her.

"If Malcolm were here, you wouldn't get away with this."

"Well, Malcolm isn't here, is he?" Thomas teased.

Malcolm, the Hutchinsons' 15-year-old Scottish indentured servant boy, was working.

"Let go, Tom," Caroline said, eyes sparkling. "Or I'll tell."

Thomas snickered. "Who are you going to tell? And who would hear you out here in the woods?"

In answer, she stomped on his big silver shoe buckle, and Thomas let out a yelp. She reached up and grabbed a handful of his thick tangle of black hair. He grabbed her arm, whirling her around so she was pinned to him, facing out and setting up a squall.

"Let me go, Tom Hutchinson! I brought Martha in the basket. She'll get you!"

Thomas hesitated for a moment. Martha the cat's claws and teeth and short temper *were* something to be reckoned with. But Martha would emerge only if Caroline let her out, Thomas knew. So he laughed and held on tighter.

Then all of a sudden she grew still. "Tom, look!" she said in a whisper.

Thomas's eyes followed the direction of her head-jerking, and he felt himself gasp.

"Isn't she beautiful?" Caroline said breathlessly.

She was—the buff-colored doe who stood in the clearing on the other side of the stream. A frail, spotted fawn next to her pounced joyfully after a butterfly.

Everything around the deer, everything around all of them, was suddenly quiet.

It hasn't felt this peaceful since the war started, Thomas thought. *Maybe if I don't move, this feeling won't all go away.*

He held his breath and stayed as still as he could. In front of him, Caroline's hair smelled like lilacs.

Suddenly, it felt funny to be noticing that. Feeling as awkward as the long-legged fawn, he let go of Caroline and gave her a push—harder than he meant to. She stumbled forward and into the brook, sitting down in the water with a soft plop.

"Tom!" she squealed. "Why did you do that, you brute?" She balled her skirts up under one arm and scrambled out of the stream after him.

"Oh, no!" Thomas cried in a high-pitched, mimicking voice. "Don't get me, Caroline!"

He gave one more shrill laugh before he took off like a musket shot through the thick woods. Caroline snatched up her basket and ran after him, hauling her wet petticoats under her arm.

Even as he hollered and spun around to let her get just beyond reach, Thomas gave a relieved sigh inside. *This feels better,* he thought. *This feels like me and Caroline.*

The chase wound through the trees, and soon Thomas was getting out of breath. Caroline was light as the deer even in soaked shoes. It wouldn't be long before she'd catch him.

Thomas looked through the trees for a hiding place to duck into. In between the September-thin leaves, he saw a big rock perched at the top of a rise. *I'll hide behind it, and it'll take her 10 minutes to find me,* Thomas thought gleefully. *She'll be so mad!*

Thomas scrambled behind the rock. As he crouched to

listen for Caroline's squishy footsteps, his eyes snagged on a sight on the other side of the rise. Before he could catch himself, he let out a slow whistle.

"I hear you, Tom Hutchinson," Caroline said from the bottom of the little slope. "I'm going to let Martha out on you."

Thomas popped up from behind the rock and motioned to her with his arm. "No, don't," he said. "Come up here!"

"Why? So you can toss me down the hill?"

"No, I won't. I promise!" he said. "Just come look at this."

She narrowed her brown eyes at him suspiciously, but she picked up the basket and scampered toward him. When she was at the top, Thomas pointed down the hill and watched as her mouth fell open.

"Oh, Tom!" she said. "I've never seen so many soldiers!"

There must have been thousands of tents pitched in the little valley below them, each with a tendril of smoke curling up from the fire in front of it. Beyond the tents, neat lines of soldiers in buff breeches and blue and red coats marched as straight as the bayonets that thrust up from their guns. Everywhere was the rat-a-tatting of drums and the piping of fifes.

It sent an eager chill up Thomas's backbone. He and his Patriot family had been waiting for six years—since 1775 when the American Revolution had first started—for enough trained soldiers to come together to face the British General Cornwallis and perhaps bring in a victory. He had watched the troops start to tramp into Williamsburg last summer, their ox-drawn wagons rumbling behind them carrying supplies and boats. Most of the soldiers had been quartered at the College of William and Mary. Now, though, there must have been 7,500 of them camped for as far as he could see.

Caroline sighed. "Patriot soldiers," she said sadly.

And Thomas knew why. Her father was a Loyalist, which meant he sided with the British in the war. She thought her brother, Alexander, was off fighting with the British Army.

Thomas swallowed hard. His own brother Sam was fighting for the Patriots. He'd written a letter home months ago telling them that Alexander was really a spy for the Americans. After his experience last summer, Thomas knew it for a fact.

He'd promised Alexander he'd never tell Caroline. The only thing he had said was that Alexander—her brother and his teacher and friend—was safe.

I wish I knew that much about my *brother,* Thomas thought as he squinted at the camp below. They hadn't heard from Sam since that letter. Papa had come into Williamsburg only once since August, because he was busy seeing to the Hutchinson's Yorktown homestead, trying to protect it from Cornwallis's men, who were preparing for battle. While he was home, he'd come to this camp looking for Sam.

But that was before all these *soldiers came,* Thomas thought. *Maybe Sam's here now.*

But he couldn't go looking for him, not with Caroline here. Her father had strictly forbidden her to go anywhere near the American military camp.

Thomas shook his head. He missed Sam so much it hurt his chest, but he wasn't going to stand here and cry in front of Caroline.

"Come on," he said to her. "We'd better go."

But she stayed still except to tug on the sleeve of his linen shirt. "Look, Tom," she said. "Something's about to happen—something big, I'll bet you."

The drum and fife music was rising to a feverish pitch,

and soldiers were dashing from their tents and gathering in rows all over the camp. Even from here, Thomas could see that a lot of these men wore shirts that hung in sweaty ribbons, and some were even barefoot—but they were standing as proudly as if they wore the scarlet breeches and high hats of the French officers who snapped smartly into place with their companies.

"Look, there's Lafayette himself," Caroline said.

"That it is, lassie," said a voice behind them.

They both whirled around to see Malcolm uncoiling his wiry form in its buckskin working breeches out from behind a bush. His tiny sister, Patsy, sprang up beside him.

"What are you two doing here?" Thomas asked.

"Sneakin' up on you two," said Malcolm, "and it isn't hard to do. Patsy and I have been behind you for five minutes."

"What's going on down there, Malcolm?" Caroline said.

Patsy scooted over and took Caroline's hand. Although Patsy was only a year younger, the little Scottish servant girl was two heads shorter, and with a dimple under each wide, innocent green eye and a charming, crooked-toothed smile, she looked even younger. The two of them gazed up at Malcolm.

Malcolm's dark, close-together eyes gleamed. "General Washington's comin', lassie."

Thomas caught his breath. "General Washington? You mean, *the* General Washington? The commander of the whole Continental Army?"

"I don't know what other General Washington I'd be talkin' about," Malcolm said dryly. "He's comin' here today to lead all these men into battle against Cornwallis at Yorktown."

"How do you know?" Thomas asked.

"The town crier brought the news just now that the general's just a few miles out," Malcolm said. "Your mama gave me leave to come and watch."

"And Mistress Lydia said I could come, too," Patsy piped up.

"We *should* be here," Malcolm said. "This is going to change our lives—Patsy's and mine. If the Patriots win this war—*when* they win it—people like us won't have to do what our betters tell us for the rest of our lives." He glanced quickly at Thomas. "Not that I'm ungrateful for what your papa's done for me, payin' to bring me here and givin' me a place to work to pay it off. But to be his equal in the eyes of the law— do you know what that means, lad?"

Thomas wasn't sure he did. He had always had the promise of that in his future. But the fire in Malcolm's eyes sent a ripple up Thomas's spine anyway. Malcolm was like another brother, especially with Sam gone to the war, and his oldest brother Clayton off in England. If it meant something to Malcolm, it was important to him, too.

"So will General Washington win this battle when he gets here, Malcolm?" Caroline was drawing a circle in the dirt with her toe. Her slice-of-melon mouth looked pinched.

"I think he will, lassie," Malcolm said. "You remember we all read in the *Gazette* just last week that that French Admiral—"

"Comte de Grasse," Thomas put in.

"—he brought his fleet into the Chesapeake Bay and launched 3,000 more troops into Jamestown. That's why you see so many men here. And with all the Allied troops gatherin' around these parts, there's about 17,000 altogether.

De Grasse is out there tryin' to ward off a British naval attack. If he wins, his ships can block off the bay so no one can send more troops and supplies to Cornwallis by sea. Now if Lafayette and Washington can take him by land—"

"Then the war will be won." Something about the sound of Caroline's voice made Thomas look at her sharply. She sounded almost like a grown-up . . . a grown-up about to cry.

"Well, now," Malcolm swaggered a little, "there's been word that Cornwallis's men have built themselves seven redoubts for guns out there in Yorktown."

"What's a redoubt?" Patsy asked.

Caroline stomped her foot. "I don't care about that!" she cried. "*Will* the Patriots win the battle?" Tears balanced on her bottom lashes.

"I was never certain before, lassie, but now with all the Allied troops gathered from all the colonies, the French army to help us, and General Washington on the way, I don't see how we can lose."

Caroline opened her mouth to say something, but a roar from the troops below sent them all scurrying to see. A group of horsemen galloped furiously onto the field, and Malcolm's arm shot out in a point.

"There he is!" he cried. "That's General Washington!"

Caroline jerked around, picked up her basket, and dashed off down the hill.

"Where are you going?" Thomas called.

She looked up at him, her brown eyes streaming. "I'm going home!" she cried. "I *hate* General Washington!"

✠ ⚜ ✠

Chapter Two

Thomas started to go after her, but Malcolm grabbed his arm.

"Let her go, lad," he said.

"Is that him, Malcolm?" Patsy was bouncing like a twirling-hoop, and Malcolm scooped her up and deposited her onto his shoulders. His face broke into its square smile.

"That's him all right. Look there, lad."

Thomas put up his hand to shield his eyes. Approaching the camp on a massive horse was a tall, broad-shouldered man in a blue and buff uniform, his auburn hair shining in the sunlight. His figure cut into the blue sky like a statue.

For the moment, Caroline slipped out of Thomas's mind.

"He's a big man, isn't he, lad?" Malcolm said. "Every shot misses him, but I don't see how."

By now the drummers were beating their instruments so fast that the sticks disappeared into a blur. But as soon as the general came in sight of the camp, a roar went up that drowned out everything else. Men shouted like boys at a game, and even the French raised their hats on their bayoneted muskets and cheered.

As the young Marquis de Lafayette galloped out to meet the general on his horse, Thomas ran his eyes over the American troops. *Sam must be down there, or at one of the other military camps around Williamsburg,* he thought. *He must be.*

Sadly, Thomas turned and looked down the rise where Caroline had long since disappeared into the woods. If this was going to be the last battle, and the Patriots won the way Malcolm said they surely would, then that meant Caroline's father's side had lost.

That's why she hates General Washington, Thomas thought. *But I suppose I would too if my father did.*

There were a lot of men Thomas looked up to and loved. There was old Francis Pickering, the apothecary he worked for in the afternoons. And Nicholas Quincy, the doctor he often went out on calls with. And of course he admired his brother Sam, even though he was a hothead, and his brother Clayton, in spite of his sometimes stuffy ways. And Alexander Taylor with his happy way of turning everything into an adventure was right up there at the top.

But there was no one Thomas regarded more highly than his father, John Hutchinson. Almost everyone felt that way about him. He was every bit as big as General Washington, and he always seemed to know what was right to do. God, Thomas had thought once, must be very good friends with John Hutchinson.

I wish he were home from the plantation now, Thomas thought. *Surely he'd be down there looking for Sam.*

"Now, those men in the homespun hunting shirts with the fringe, those are the riflemen," Malcolm was saying.

"What do you suppose Sam would be wearing?" Thomas asked.

Malcolm narrowed his black eyes at him. "Are you searchin' for him, lad?"

Thomas shrugged. "Maybe."

"It's sure he'll not come home lookin' for your papa," Malcolm said. "Not as mad as your father was at him for runnin' off and joinin' the army when he forbid him to do it." Malcolm shook his shaggy black head. "Though I can't say as I blame the lad. Lookin' down at this scene, I'm wishin' I was part of it myself."

Thomas felt his mouth drop open. "You? You want to join the army, too?"

"Well, who wouldn't?" Malcolm said. He nodded toward the troops below who were all standing at impressive attention while their general passed among them, touching shoulders and shaking hands with even the most bedraggled. "They say deserters are common," Malcolm said in a voice like a prayer, "but woe be unto any deserter I ever catch. It's a privilege to serve under such a man."

"But are you thinking of going?" Thomas said. His heart was slamming inside his chest.

"No. Don't go *anywhere!*" Patsy cried. She squeezed Malcolm's neck until his thin face went scarlet.

"You're chokin' me, lassie!" Malcolm said. He tugged gently at one of her black braids. "They wouldn't take me anyway. I'm but 15, and you have to be 16 to serve."

Thomas's heart stopped hammering, and he let out a slow sigh. It was all right again. He wasn't sure he could take another of his "brothers" leaving.

"It looks like he'll be movin' on to the next camp,"

Malcolm said, his eyes still glued to General Washington. "I'd like to follow a ways. You comin', lad?"

Thomas shook his head. "I promised Mr. Pickering I would go to the hospital to see if Dr. Quincy needs anything."

Malcolm shifted Patsy on his back and started down the rise with Thomas beside him. "If you can call what they have set up in the old Governor's Palace a hospital," he said. "Esther sent me over there with some soup yesterday, and the stench nearly drove me out."

"It isn't Nicholas's fault!" Thomas said fiercely.

"Of course not. He's one person against all those feet full of sores and runnin' blisters full of dirt."

"Ugh, Malcolm stop!" said Patsy.

"And the battle hasn't even begun yet," Malcolm went on as they started through the woods. "They say livin' in these camps causes more sufferin' than the fightin' does."

"Then no wonder there are deserters," Thomas started to say.

"Shhh!" Malcolm said sharply.

Thomas froze behind Malcolm and pricked up his ears. There was a faint rustling in the trees just beyond them.

"Caroline and I did see deer around here a little while ago," Thomas whispered.

Malcolm shook his head and silently slid Patsy off his back. "It was a soldier I saw," he whispered.

"A soldier?" Thomas whispered back. He crashed behind Malcolm into the trees. Patsy caught up and grabbed her brother's hand. "What's a soldier doing out here?" Thomas said.

"Deserting would be my guess," Malcolm said between his tightened teeth. "But not after I get hold of him."

He put his finger to his lips. Thomas and Patsy listened

with him. The rustling stopped, close by. Malcolm shot them a warning look that said *Stay here* and moved toward the noise. For a moment there wasn't a sound. Then suddenly Malcolm sprang to life and dove behind a white-barked sycamore. The whole tree shook, and birds scattered in all directions, screaming out startled squawks as they were rattled from their perches. Malcolm was shrieking loudest of all.

"I got you, you miserable coward! You were runnin' away, weren't you? Weren't you?"

Patsy locked her arms around Thomas's leg and dug her face into the brown cloth of his breeches. Malcolm was spitting out words as if they were snake venom as he hauled out a slender figure by the back of his shirt.

It was a soldier all right, wearing the homespun breeches and oversized tricornered hat Malcolm had said showed he was a rifleman. But Thomas saw at once that he wasn't carrying a gun, rifle or otherwise, unless it was tucked under the too-big coat the soldier had on, even in the humid warmth of Virginia September.

Malcolm had obviously thought of a gun, too, because he sent the soldier sprawling to the ground and pounced on him, then threw open the coat and began to poke at the lining. The soldier held on to his hat and whimpered.

"Where's your weapon, soldier?" Malcolm demanded.

"I don't have one," the soldier said in a husky voice. "I never did!"

Thomas decided he couldn't be much older than Malcolm himself.

"Do you take me for a fool?" Malcolm shouted at him as he turned him over on his stomach and patted his breeches. "A soldier without a weapon? No, you sold it to get money so you could get home. I know your kind!"

"No, you don't!" the soldier cried in a voice muffled by the hat he still held on to his head and the dirt his face was stuck into.

The way Malcolm was sitting on him clawing at his clothes, Thomas felt almost sorry for the boy. *He's probably wishing he* hadn't *deserted,* Thomas thought.

"You don't know my kind at all!" the soldier cried again. He wriggled desperately under Malcolm's sinewy frame. "Let me up and I'll explain!"

Malcolm rose just enough to flip the boy over and plopped down on his stomach. The soldier clung to the hat that dipped down over his eyes and lay there, breathing hard. By now, Patsy had pulled one of the buckles loose at the knee of Thomas's breeches, she was hanging on to him so hard. It looked as if Malcolm were about to shoot flames out of his nostrils.

"So," he said hotly, "explain!"

"I'm not a deserter—"

"Then where's your company?"

"I don't have one—"

"Liar! Every soldier has a company!"

"I'm not a soldier!"

There was a stunned silence for a second before Malcolm shouted, "You have the *nerve* to wear the proud uniform of a Patriot soldier when you don't even serve in the American army?" The soldier didn't seem to know whether to shake his head or nod, and Malcolm didn't give him a chance. "You don't deserve to wear it!" he shouted again. "So take it off. No, wait! I'm going to rip it off of you, you lousy impostor!"

Patsy screamed and hid behind Thomas's knees. Malcolm

reached down for the tricornered hat and gave it a rip.

It came off, and out spilled a tangle of long, reddish hair.

It took Thomas a moment to realize the soldier was a woman.

It didn't take Malcolm that long. He shot up like a cannonball and stood looking down at her in horror and breathing like a bull.

Thomas had to cover his mouth with his hand to keep from laughing.

"Malcolm!" Patsy said as she peeked out from behind Thomas's leg. "It's a lady!"

"I know it's a lady," Malcolm snapped. "I'm not stupid."

"Well, you could have fooled me."

That came from the "soldier," who was collecting her hat from the ground and getting to her feet.

"It would only have taken a smart person that long—" she snapped her fingers "—to figure out he was wrestling a female."

"I'm sorry, ma'am!" Malcolm said.

He looked as if he were about to be shot. Thomas expected him to put both hands up in surrender any minute.

"You *should* be sorry," the woman said.

Thomas watched as she brushed the grass and leaves from her jacket. He was fascinated by her hands. Unlike his mother's delicate, china-white hands, these were chapped and ruddy-red, and the knuckles were as thick as his own. He wasn't sure any of the female servants on their plantation had hands that looked as if they'd worked as hard as this lady's.

She stopped brushing off her jacket and looked up to see Thomas staring at her. "What are *you* looking at?" she said.

"I . . . I was just—" Thomas stammered.

"I know," she cut in. "You were just thinking that it was no wonder this wildcat didn't notice I was of the female persuasion because my disguise was so clever. Was that it?"

There was something about the crisp way she said it that made Thomas nod his head. Everything about her was crisp—her gray-blue eyes, her busy eyebrows, the way she pulled her deer-colored hair back into its braid. She was taller than most of the women Thomas knew, and she had a husky voice.

It wasn't the disguise that led us to believe you were a man, Thomas thought. *It was you!*

After all, he mused, he'd seen a girl dressed up like a boy before. Caroline had pulled that trick on him several times. And he himself had had to wear a dress once—

"Close your mouth, boy, or you'll be catching flies," the woman said.

She was talking to Malcolm, who was still gaping at her in disbelief. He closed his lips obediently, and then opened them again to say, "I'm sorry . . . I didn't mean to . . . is there somewhere I can take you? . . . I mean, to make up for—"

"Yes," she said as she briskly shook off the heavy coat she no longer needed to hide her slender figure. "You can take me to a man I've come looking for, if you know him."

"What's his name?" Malcolm asked.

"Nicholas Quincy," she said. "Dr. Nicholas Quincy."

✢ ⋅✢⋅ ✢

Chapter Three

ll three of their mouths fell open. Patsy was the first to come out of her stupor.

"We know Dr. Quincy!" she cried. "He's our friend!"

The woman's eyes flicked back to Malcolm. "I find it hard to believe that the Nicholas Quincy I know would be friends with the likes of this brute."

"Beggin' your pardon, lassie," Malcolm said, "but I doubt the Nicholas Quincy we know would be friends with a woman who pretends to be a soldier."

"My name is Winifred deWindt. I come from Pennsylvania."

"That *is* where Nicholas comes from, Malcolm," Thomas said.

"Of course that's where he comes from," Winifred said. "We grew up together. When I heard that the battle was about to start in these parts, I knew he'd be in some makeshift hospital down here, trying to save men from a war he doesn't think they should be fighting in the first place."

"That's only because he's a Quaker," Malcolm said.

"Now is that a fact?"

Thomas could almost hear her eyes snapping.

"I'm aware that he's a Quaker, sonny," she said. "I'm one myself."

Malcolm's face was blotchy with embarrassment. "Then why were you wearin' a uniform?" he asked, his voice bristling.

"Because that's the only safe way for a woman to travel alone these days." Winifred shot her sharp eyes down at Patsy. "And you remember that, missy."

Patsy dove for Thomas's pant leg again, and Thomas continued to stare at Winifred. He'd never seen a woman quite like her. None of the women he knew ever acted as if she had things to do so you'd better get out of the way, the way this lady did.

"What are *you* laughing at?"

Thomas's thoughts shot back to Winifred's crisp blue-gray eyes. He put his hand up and wiped off the grin that had sneaked onto his face. Winifred turned to Malcolm.

"Now if you'll tell me where I can find Nicholas Quincy, I'll be on my way."

"We'll show you," Malcolm said glumly.

We must be a funny sight, Thomas thought as the four of them made their way across the ridge toward the College of William and Mary, which sat at one end of Williamsburg. *A funny sight indeed with Malcolm strutting along like the chief rooster and me following behind with Patsy hanging on to my pant leg and this soldier in a hat that's too big for him— only he's not a him, he's a her!*

They passed the college and headed down the Duke of Gloucester Street, turning off at the Palace Green. As they went by Thomas's house, which faced the Green, he wondered what his mother and their old nurse Esther would think if they happened to look out the sitting room window, or if old Otis, Esther's husband, was crossing the yard and saw them.

Or what if Caroline saw us? Thomas thought gleefully. Her house was just around the corner on Nicholson Street. *She would surely have something clever to say to Winifred.* Then he suddenly got sad when he thought, *What if now that Caroline's father's side might lose, he won't let her play with us anymore?*

But there was no time to stew over that. They'd reached the big brick building at the end of the Green, which at one time had been the Palace for the Royal Governors of the King of England before the war for Independence started. After that the American governors had lived there. And then it had been empty for a while, when Thomas had first been sent from the plantation to Williamsburg to live and Thomas Jefferson had just moved the capital of Virginia to Richmond. That was when Thomas and Caroline would go to the gardens behind the Palace and play every evening, especially on the Chinese Bridge.

Thomas sighed as they went through the heavy front door. There was nothing imaginary about it anymore. It was now a hospital for the Patriot soldiers, and everything about it was very real, including the smell. He held his breath as he followed Malcolm and Winifred inside.

"What is that stench?" Malcolm muttered, pinching his nose.

"That, sonny, is the smell of sickness," Winifred said. "If there's going to be a battle, there will be enough of it to smell up the whole town. Get used to it."

"Thank you," Malcolm said with an edge in his voice. "I'll work on it."

Thomas unpeeled Patsy from his leg, and she shot over

to Malcolm. She gave Winifred one long, frightened gaze before she tugged at her brother's sleeve.

"We'll be goin' now," he said.

But Winifred ignored him and pointed her sharp eyes at Thomas. "Well, then, where's Nicholas, sonny?"

"Me?" Thomas said.

"No, I'm talking to that candle stand. Of course you! I thought you said you knew him."

"I do!" Thomas said.

That quickly, the back of his neck started to prickle. Malcolm was gone, and she was bossing him now—and it wasn't funny anymore.

I hope she's not staying long, Thomas thought irritably.

He looked around for Nicholas, but at the moment, all he saw were two long rows of pallets on the floor, each holding a sick soldier. The only person standing up was his friend and boss Francis Pickering, who was walking stiffly from one man to the next, handing out troches, syrups, and tinctures.

Thomas smiled impishly to himself. *I ought to tell her that's Nicholas, and that the hard work of caring for the soldiers has aged him before his time.*

"That has to be the apothecary," Winifred said. "They all get that hump in their backs from hunching over the mortar and pestle for hours at a time. I'd know one anywhere."

So much for that trick, Thomas thought. To Winifred he said, "I'll go look for Nicholas in the back room."

"Do it then," she said brusquely and waved him off.

Thomas hurried off down the aisle between the rows of pallets and was almost to the doorway when a voice shouted at him.

"You there! Hutchinson! Come over here!"

Thomas froze in midstep. It couldn't be. But no one else in the world had a voice that sounded as if it were being squeezed out of a set of bagpipes. It had to be Xavier Wormeley.

Thomas hadn't seen the fat, floppy-jowled militiaman for months, and he didn't want to see him now. Even back when he was a magistrate in Williamsburg, Xavier had made no end of trouble for the Hutchinsons and the Taylors. Thomas thought he'd seen the last of Xavier in the spring when he'd nearly had Nicholas hanged.

Thomas turned slowly and looked down at the pallet at his feet. There he was, peering out of his poke-hole eyes and flapping his jowls as he barked out, "Hutchinson! I said get over here!"

What's he doing here? Thomas thought wildly. *He doesn't look sick.*

He wanted to run, but once more Xavier shrilled out his name in his organ-pipe voice and sent a jolt through Thomas that bolted him to the floor.

"I'm a sick man!" Wormeley cried. "Why can't I get anyone to help me?"

"There's no one free to help you," Thomas said, trying to get his feet unstuck from the floorboards.

"You're here, Hutchinson. Get me some tea at once!"

"Good heavens, man, pipe down." Winifred was suddenly at Thomas's elbow, and she brushed past him and crouched down beside Xavier Wormeley. Her piercing gaze sliced through him long enough for him to stare back—and shut up. She shook her head and stood up briskly. "Every man in here is worse off than you are," she said. "I'll thank you to keep your voice down and let them rest."

Xavier's face turned crimson as he gathered his breath for

the next bellow. But Winifred nipped it in the first note.

"Don't get yourself all in a dither, because it will do you no good," she said and turned away.

"And *who* might *you* be?" Xavier shouted.

"The name's Winifred. Winifred deWindt," she said without turning around to face him. "My friends call me Winnie. You may call me Winifred."

That faint twinkle that Thomas had seen before came over her face again as she moved away. Thomas smothered a grin. Beside them, someone groaned softly.

"Mademoiselle?" said the man on the next pallet. He murmured something in French.

Winifred dropped to her knees and looked into the face that barely peeked out from behind a wild brown beard.

"What do you need, soldier?" Winifred said to him.

Thomas stared. The voice that was coming out of her was not the same voice he'd been hearing since he'd met her. This voice was soothing and rich, like good pudding. He watched in amazement as she smoothed one big, rough hand over the blanket and the other across the man's forehead.

"Let me get you some soup," she said. She cocked her head up at Thomas like a little bird. "Sonny—"

A shout erupted from Xavier Wormeley's pallet. *"What?* I ask for something and you tell me to shut it. This Frenchman whimpers and he has an entire team at his disposal!"

"That's right, Jowls," Winifred said. "A few days without food and you'll start to feel a lot better. Well, sonny, how about that soup?"

Thomas chewed at the inside of his mouth to keep laughter from busting out and turned on his heel. He took two steps and ran smack into a tall lanky man with rolled-up sleeves and a trembly mouth.

"Dr. Quincy!" Thomas said. "We found a friend of yours."

But Nicholas had already seen her. He was staring over Thomas's head, and his face was working like a butter churn.

"Winnie," he said.

"Nicholas Quincy, why hasn't this man been given liquids?" Winifred said briskly. Then she nodded toward Xavier and said, "And why hasn't this one been booted out of here?"

She stood up, and Nicholas flew straight into her arms and lifted her off her feet.

"Winnie!" Nicholas said. "Winnie, Winnie, Winnie."

Yeah, that's her name, Thomas thought as he watched them sway back and forth in a hug that lasted longer than *conversations* Thomas had had. He squirmed and looked away.

"Amour," said the little Frenchman with the big beard.

"What does that mean?" Xavier growled at him. "If you're going to serve in this country, learn to speak the language."

Nicholas pulled himself gently away from Winnie and held her at arm's length. He stared into her face, and she stared into his until Thomas couldn't watch it anymore.

"I'll go get some soup," he said.

With his head spinning, he hurried into the room where they kept the food supplies. *Nicholas never mentioned Winifred before,* he thought. *He never mentioned any girl— especially not one that acts like a general.*

"What are you about there, Hutchinson?"

Thomas looked up from the vat of soup hanging over the fireplace to see Francis Pickering tottering toward him. The old man coughed and then peered over his spectacles.

"Getting soup, sir," Thomas said.

"Who is that woman Nicholas is making eyes at out there?" Francis said.

"He's not making eyes at her!"

Francis grunted. "You're an infant, Hutchinson. When you get to be as old as I am, you know what making eyes looks like. Who is she?"

"Her name's Winifred," Thomas said glumly as he scooped soup into a tin mug. "She's from Pennsylvania."

"Ah," Francis said, jerking his half-bald head as if he had it all figured out already. "So she dressed up in that soldier's get-up so she could get here on her own to see her man."

"He's not her man!" Thomas said.

"What difference does it make to you if he is or isn't, Hutchinson?" Francis asked.

Thomas couldn't answer that. *And it doesn't matter anyway,* he told himself. *She'll visit for a few days and then she'll go back to Pennsylvania. It's sure I don't want her around here, bossing me around.*

Francis eased himself into a chair and coughed as he watched Thomas. "Things change awful fast when you're growing up," he said.

Thomas didn't know what he was talking about and he didn't care. He hung up the ladle and headed for the door with the cup of soup.

"Hutchinson," Francis said, "take some of these ginger troches to the Frenchman, will you? I'm too tired to make that walk again."

Thomas nodded absently and took the cough drops in his hand. It was probably safe to go out there now. Maybe they'd be finished hugging by now.

But although they'd moved away from Xavier Wormeley's

pallet, Nicholas and Winnie were still holding on to each other's hands and looking into each other's eyes.

Thomas stomped past the gooey-eyed couple, making as much noise as he could, and knelt down next to the Frenchman. "Here's your soup, sir," he said.

The Frenchman's eyes fluttered open, and he smiled out of his briar-patch beard. "Ah, *merci,*" he said.

"Shall I leave it right here?" Thomas asked.

The soldier suddenly looked ashamed.

"You'll have to feed it to him, sonny," Winifred said in her starched voice. "He can't even sit up."

"Oh, and what am *I* to do?" Xavier Wormeley whined. He sat bolt upright on his pallet, and Thomas noticed for the first time that his hair was oiled and powdered and tied into a perfect queue. He wore a royal purple bed jacket with lace on the sleeves.

"You?" Winnie said to him. "You ought to get out of that sickbed and feed him."

The Frenchman laughed softly. "No, mademoiselle," he said, and pointed to her.

"Then it's me who shall help you," she said crisply. She marched over, her reddish braid bobbing against her back in a businesslike way, and arched her eyebrows at Thomas.

"Ma'am?" Thomas said.

"Move out of the way, sonny," she said. "I have a patient to feed. I'm working here now."

✠ ⋅✠⋅ ✠

Chapter Four

Winifred's announcement was met with silent stares—until Xavier all but sprang from his pallet to protest.

"Working *here?*" he shouted, jowls quivering madly. "By whose orders?"

Usually Thomas disagreed with Xavier Wormeley, but this time he found himself nodding in agreement.

"I don't need anyone's orders," she said. "But if you need someone's approval, you can ask the doctor."

All eyes shifted to Nicholas Quincy. He looked more pale and awkward than ever. A blotch of embarrassed red appeared on each cheek.

"You, Quincy?" Xavier boomed. "You brought a woman in here—to a *military* site?"

Nicholas looked at Winnie helplessly. "Now, Winnie, I didn't say—"

"You didn't have to!" She swept her arm across the sickroom. "One look at this place and it's obvious you need help.

You've all *you* can do just to take care of the worst cases—the pneumonia and smallpox and such. And that apothecary's so old he looks like he should be bedded down himself."

Thomas scowled at her. Everyone knew that Francis was the best apothecary in all of Virginia. Who was she to question him?

"So who's going to feed all these sick men? And get them clean bed linens? And keep the odor in here down where a person can breathe?" She directed her crisp gaze on Xavier. "You're going to get a bevy of *men* in here to do all that? I daresay you won't find even one who's willing." Her eyes sprang back to Nicholas, who to Thomas's dismay was softening around the lips. "If you tell me to go packing back to Pennsylvania, Nicholas Quincy, you know I will. But you can't deny you need me here."

Thomas fixed his own deep-set Hutchinson blue eyes on Dr. Quincy and silently begged him to tell her no.

Nicholas did shake his head. "You know you can't lift—"

"I've got the boy here to help me!"

Thomas was looking around to see what boy she was talking about when Nicholas sighed and took her hands.

"You're right, Winnie," he said. "As always, you're right."

What? Thomas almost shouted at him. *She's right? No! Don't let her stay here! She'll ruin everything!*

Xavier's jowls were working double-time. "You mean, she's to stay here and nurse . . . soldiers?" he cried.

"That she is, Xavier," Nicholas said. "And you won't find a better nurse in the colonies." The embarrassed blotches had disappeared, and he was looking like his confident doctor-self again. His eyes even shone as he said, "She'll have you out of here in no time."

"Oh, you can count on that," Winnie said. She rubbed her hands together as if she couldn't wait to get started on that task. "Sonny," she said to Thomas, "let's have some more of that soup."

Getting rid of Xavier Wormeley is the only good thing I can think of about her staying here, Thomas thought as he made his way toward the food room again. But behind him he heard the Frenchman gibber a bunch of French, with the English word angels thrown in.

"It wasn't angels that brought her here," Thomas muttered as he pushed open the door. "It was us. And wait till Malcolm finds out what we've done!"

"Don't start talking to yourself this early on, Hutchinson," Francis said, "or you'll have nothing left to say when you get to be my age."

"Yes, sir," Thomas mumbled.

Old Francis peered at him curiously. "Who put that sour look on your face?"

But before he could answer, Winifred's voice shouted from the other room. "You there—apothecary! Can we have some licorice root and ginseng out here for these boys? And quickly?"

Thomas cocked an eyebrow at the old man. Francis cocked one back.

"Ah, I see," Francis said.

In all the months Thomas had worked for Francis Pickering, he had never spent an afternoon longer than that one. It was growing dark when he was finally allowed to leave.

Every time he tried, Winifred deWindt shouted across the ballroom, "Where do you think you're going, sonny? That soldier in the corner needs to be fed!" or "Not so fast, sonny. Who do you think is going to clean up that mess in the kitchen?" or "Hold on, sonny! That man there needs some columbine leaves for that sore mouth. Who do you think is going to get them, eh?" And not once had he gotten to work beside Nicholas, the way he usually did.

I'd probably still be there if I hadn't sneaked out, he told himself as he finally headed through the shadows toward the Hutchinsons' house. He'd seen his chance when Winnie had stopped to hold hands with Dr. Quincy in a corner again. *Although the way they were looking at each other,* he thought, *I could have left and taken half the beds with me, and they'd never have known!*

It was beyond him what they were looking at. Nicholas Quincy was one of his favorite people in the world, but he was nothing much to see with his pale, almost no-color eyes, his round, quivering lips, and the way he had of almost cowering when he wasn't doctoring.

But Winifred, she was even less of an eye-pleaser as far as Thomas could see. Not that Thomas had ever thought very much about what women looked like. Wasn't this lady kind of rough and untidy, what with her hair bristling out of that braid at all angles and her face getting all hard like a pecan when she was concentrating? Thomas thought of her rough hands and the husky way she barked out orders.

As Thomas wiped his feet on the back steps, he shrugged. *I guess it doesn't matter to Nicholas what she looks like. She's just his assistant—*

The thought stopped him cold with his hand on the doorknob.

She was his assistant?

But what about me? Thomas thought. *I've been the one helping him ever since he came here! Why does he need her?*

The idea bristled up his spine as if porcupine quills were coming to attention.

"You can't *think* the door open," said a voice at the bottom of the steps. "You have to turn the knob."

"I know," Thomas growled over his shoulder at Malcolm.

He pushed open the door, and Malcolm followed him inside with an armload of wood.

"Had a bad time of it at the hospital, did you?" Malcolm said with a gleam in his eyes.

"Yes, I did," Thomas snapped at him. "And wait until you find out why."

They moved into the dining room, where the table was set for supper and the fireplace awaited Malcolm's wood. He set it down on the hearth and looked quizzically at Thomas.

"Well?"

"That Winifred woman," Thomas said. "She's going to stay here and work at the hospital with Dr. Quincy."

A scowl darkened Malcolm's merry face. "For how long?"

"For as long as he needs her."

Malcolm's frown deepened, and Thomas nodded. But then Malcolm smiled his square smile.

"That's really no skin off my nose, lad," he said. "I'm done with her. But you—" he jabbed a finger playfully into Thomas's chest "—you are the one who is going to have to work with her every day. I'll wager she can give out the orders, eh?"

It was Thomas's turn to scowl, and he did until he could see his own eyebrows scrunched over his eyes. "She was even bossing old Francis around!"

Malcolm grinned. "That won't last long."

"Oh, and guess who else is at the hospital, as a patient? Xavier Wormeley."

Malcolm let out a long, slow whistle, eyes still twinkling with mischief. "I guess you're in for a bad run of it now, lad. I don't envy you."

"I just won't go," Thomas said stubbornly as he followed Malcolm out of the dining room and toward the back door.

"Won't go where?" a deep voice said.

Both boys gave a startled jolt and stared down the back hall. Just emerging from his library office was tall John Hutchinson.

"Papa!" Thomas cried.

He shoved Malcolm aside and dashed toward his father. Papa caught him in a hug and tousled his black hair.

"By the way, lad," Malcolm said, chuckling as he went out the back door. "I forgot to tell you, your papa's come home."

Thomas barely heard him as he looked up at his father's lined, sturdy face. "I didn't know you were coming today!"

"I couldn't miss General Washington's entrance into Virginia, could I?"

Thomas shook his head happily. Suddenly, nothing else mattered much. When Papa was with them, everything always felt as if it were going to work out somehow.

A lumpy figure bustled down the stairs, followed by a brush of linen skirts. Esther bobbed to the bottom step with Mama at her heels, and she was, as usual, chattering the whole way.

"All right, all right!" the old woman clucked. "Cook says dinner is on its way. It's time you all got to the table."

"I won't argue with that," Papa said as he took his wife's

arm. "But then, I never have argued with you, Esther."

Thomas held back a snort as he followed them into the dining room. Esther had not only been his nurse when he was a little boy, and Sam's and Clayton's before him, but she'd also taken care of their father when he was a child. She'd been giving all of them orders since they were old enough to crawl.

At least now she's just Mama's companion and isn't in charge of me anymore, Thomas thought. Esther was loyal to them all, and he loved her because . . . well, because she was Esther. But the fewer people he had bossing him around, the better.

In the dining room, Thomas eyed the table hungrily. It seemed to be groaning under the weight of potatoes and squash and pumpkin bread and meats. He sniffed as Malcolm placed a tureen right in the center.

"Rabbit stew," Malcolm murmured and then slipped out of the dining room.

"So what have you been up to, my dear?" Papa said across the table. His deep-set blue Hutchinson eyes were twinkling at his wife.

Virginia Hutchinson's gray eyes shone back at him, and her black curls, so much like Thomas's in color, danced around her pretty face.

"John," she said proudly, "I have learned to spin flax! Several of the ladies in town have brought their wheels and we've set them up in the parlor and spun our little hearts out! And of course, for every dress or cape we make for ourselves, we make five garments for the soldiers."

"You've been a wonder, my dear, rallying the women to support the war effort." Papa's eyes were admiring. "Your help is much appreciated. And you look just as beautiful in homespun linen as you always have in silk."

They gazed over the steaming food at each other, and Thomas squirmed. *Why is everybody staring at each other like a bunch of idiots all of a sudden?* he thought. He shook the image of Nicholas and Winnie locking eyeballs out of his mind and reached for his silver tankard full of apple cider.

"I only wish there were more we could do," Virginia Hutchinson said finally. "Especially with the battle coming. It is coming, isn't it, John?"

Papa's face was suddenly somber. "Cornwallis's men are working day and night, building up their fortification. They lured black slaves away from the plantations and forced them to dig their walls and trenches in that scorching August heat, even in the middle of the day. They had men dying out there, and the battle's not yet begun!"

The Look had formed on Papa's face—the one in which his eyebrows knitted into a knot, his mouth pressed into a stern line, and his eyes drilled into the unfortunate person on the receiving end. Papa leaned back in his side chair and gazed into the flickering fire. "I always thought we could have our independence without it costing all these lives. It seems I was wrong."

Mama sat straight up in her chair. "Well, then, if there must be a battle, we have no other choice but to win it."

"You're right, of course, dear," Papa said. "But it is not at all a certainty."

"Malcolm says it is!" Thomas said.

Papa pierced his eyes at him. "Does Malcolm have some information the rest of us are not privy to?"

"I don't know, sir," Thomas said nervously. "He only told me that Comte de Grasse has a fleet of French ships out in the Chesapeake Bay to cut off Cornwallis's supplies."

"If the comte can hold back the resistance he's getting from the British Navy," Papa said sharply. "But if he fails to hold them, it will mean disaster."

There was a hard silence for a moment, but Mama cut into it with an abrupt, "Well."

"Well what, my dear?" Papa said.

"There is only one thing to do, and that is to gather the women for prayer. We must get on our knees on the part of this Comte de Grasse!" She pressed her ruffled wrists against the table and pushed her chair back. "I must begin to send messages to the ladies right away."

Papa's face smoothed again as he reached over and put one of his big hands on one of her tiny ones. "I think that's an excellent idea, my love," he said. "But can it wait until after we've had dessert?"

Thomas sniffed automatically. "It's apple tarts. They're coming now."

The air was calm again by the time Malcolm brought in the tray of tarts and set them on the table. He twitched an eyebrow at Thomas before he turned to stoke the fire, and Thomas knew he'd already sampled one.

"If I'm to keep you here until the cloth is drawn," Papa said, his eyes twinkling at Mama, "I had better change the subject. I have had a letter from Clayton."

Mama squealed, the war obviously forgotten already. "Is he well?" she said. "Has he been ordained? Does he know when he's coming home?"

Papa laughed as he put his hand up. "Only three questions at a time! He is well. That smallpox vaccine Nicholas gave him is evidently working, and so is his heart.

We must have Nicholas to dinner and thank him again."

"Tomorrow," Mama said. "I'll tell Cook."

"Clayton has been ordained," Papa went on. "He is now a minister in the Church of England, though what his place will be when he comes back to a country that is no longer under the rule of England is still anyone's guess—"

"And when will he be home?" Mama asked.

"That I cannot answer, my dear. Things being what they are, it may be safer for him to wait until the war is over to try to return."

"Then we must pray not only for a victory, but for a *quick* victory," Mama said firmly. "I must get word to the prayers. Will you gentlemen excuse me?"

When she was gone, John Hutchinson shook his head. "If any harm were to come to any of you boys, your mother would never be the same. That's why she fights so hard."

"Sir, has there been a letter from Sam, too?" Thomas said.

Papa shook his head again and then reached inside his waistcoat. "The only other mail was this," he said. He pulled out a square box wrapped in brown paper and handed it to Thomas, who stared at it blankly. Malcolm looked over curiously from the fireplace.

"What is it?" Thomas asked.

"Something I ordered for you from Philadelphia. They still have the finest craftsmen there."

Thomas tore open the paper and pulled the lid from the box. Lying in the bottom was a shiny leather pouch attached to an equally handsome belt. Thomas looked up at his father, baffled.

"It's a money pouch," Papa said. "I know you have no money, but you'll find some use for it, I'm sure. Stand up."

Thomas did, and Papa took the belted pouch from the box and fitted it around Thomas's waist. "It gives you the look of a young man," he said. He gave the belt a final cinch.

Thomas nodded numbly and said, "Thank you, sir."

"I never had a chance to do this with Sam," Papa said. His voice was thick. "And perhaps I never shall."

Thomas felt his heart sinking.

"It has been months since we have heard from Sam," Papa said, "and all my inquiries here have turned up nothing."

"But there are new soldiers here now!" Thomas said.

"I checked today." John Hutchinson shook his head. "We can continue to hope, of course. But there is a chance, Thomas, that your brother will not come home again."

☦ ⸱☦⸱ ☦

Chapter Five

"We'll have Evening Prayer in the parlor in a few minutes," Papa said.

Thomas didn't answer. Even when his father quietly left the room, he sat staring at the tabletop with Papa's words lying motionless in his mind.

"I'm sorry, lad."

Thomas's head jerked up. He'd forgotten Malcolm was still there, crouched by the fireplace.

"Sorry about what?" Thomas said woodenly.

"About Sam. I didn't know him well—"

"Then you'll get to know him!" Thomas said fiercely. "When he comes back!"

Malcolm stood up and moved slowly to the table where Thomas still sat, drilling his eyes into the salt dish.

"Your father just said—"

"He's wrong."

Malcolm stopped beside him. "Your father?"

"Yes. It could happen, you know!"

"But he seems to have such doubts—"

"I don't care! He's *wrong!*"

"All right, all right!" Malcolm put his hands up.

Thomas blinked hard. "He can't be dead!"

"Do you think he is?"

"He can't be!"

Malcolm glanced carefully over his shoulder and then sank into the chair next to Thomas. "I know you don't want him to be dead, but do you think he is? Do you feel it in here, lad?" Malcolm tapped Thomas on the chest, and Thomas shook his head, still batting back the tears.

"It doesn't hurt inside, like it does when something bad happens," Thomas said.

"You'd know if he was really gone," Malcolm said.

Thomas nodded.

"I wonder if Caroline ever wonders whether Alexander is still alive," Malcolm said.

Thomas bit his lip to keep from blurting out, *He is alive! I know he is!* Instead, he said, "She sure hates General Washington."

"I don't think she does," Malcolm said. He picked up an empty tray and headed for the door.

"Why not?" Thomas said as he followed him out of the dining room. "She said so."

"She just hates what losing the war is going to mean for her family."

Thomas chewed on that as they went out the back door and stopped on the porch. "Don't you think people will forget they were on the losing side after a while?" he said.

Malcolm stared at him. "Do you think that's all that's going to happen to the Taylors when the Patriots win this war?"

Thomas wriggled uneasily. "Isn't that right?"

"No, lad, it isn't right. It's going to be a good bit worse than that."

"But what—?"

"Thomas," said a deep voice from the door behind them. "Come in for Evening Prayer and then it's off to bed with you. We have an early morning tomorrow."

Thomas turned to face his father. "Early? Where are we going?"

"Several of the barges I've had made for the Army are finished. I'm going down to the James River to see that they've been delivered, and I would like for you to go with me."

As Papa closed the door, Thomas turned to Malcolm with the questions crowding to be asked. *Did you hear that? I'll see the soldiers near Jamestown! Do you think Sam is there?* But Malcolm had already gone out to the kitchen building, and Thomas could hear the voices joining for Evening Prayer inside.

I've got my own prayers to pray tonight, Thomas thought as he went in. *God, You have to help me find Sam and prove Papa wrong.*

The roosters weren't even crowing yet when they headed out, Papa on Judge, his big bay, and Thomas on Burgess, the Hutchinsons' other bay. The predawn fog seemed to swallow them up as they rode toward the James River.

Thomas yawned noisily when they passed the College of William and Mary. It was almost hard to remember when the lawn had been dotted with students in black gowns dashing for class. Now the building was bulging with soldiers who were waiting for battle.

Sam has now been both, Thomas thought. *And he'll come back and finish school. I know he will.*

Papa cleared his throat. "As soon as this wretched war is over, we are going to concentrate on your education again, Thomas. I need a Hutchinson who is prepared to take over the plantation someday."

"What about Sam?" Thomas asked.

He could see the muscles in his father's jaw tightening and his knuckles growing white around the reins. Papa didn't answer.

That's all right, Thomas thought. *He'll see.*

They didn't say much else as they made their way south and the sun burned through the sleepy fog. By the time they reached the boggy fields near the James River, they could plainly see the military camps waking up all around them and hear the sounds of another anxious day beginning.

Thomas leaned out as far as he dared as they passed.

All we need is just one glimpse of Sam, he thought.

"Whoa there!" a soldier in blue and buff called out to them. He shifted his gun importantly on his shoulder and strode up as Papa reined in Judge and Thomas stopped on the other side of him.

"Have you official business here, sir?" the soldier asked.

Yes! Thomas wanted to shout to him. *We're looking for Samuel Hutchinson. Have you see him?*

"I do," Papa said politely. He pulled some papers from his money pouch.

He explained their errand, and Thomas turned and craned his neck again. The camp was alive with activity as men cleaned their guns and tended their fires and—

Thomas's eyes started open. There was a young soldier . . .

with blond hair . . . like Sam's . . . sitting on the ground outside his tent. . . .

Thomas gasped, and the soldier looked up—and Thomas felt himself deflate. It wasn't Sam. This boy was younger, perhaps closer to Malcolm's age, and he didn't have the Hutchinson broad soldiers or the fire in his eyes.

All Thomas could see in this boy's eyes was pain. He was unwrapping a strip of dirty cloth from his foot and gritting his teeth as he tugged at the last of it to get it unstuck from the bottom of his foot. Thomas saw why. Square in the middle of the sole was an angry-looking sore that oozed blood and some white stuff that made Thomas grimace. He'd dressed a lot of sores with Francis and Dr. Quincy, but he'd never seen anything that looked as bad as that.

He remembered Winifred saying, *"And the battle hasn't even started yet."*

Papa finished his discussion with the soldier, picked up the reins, and clicked his tongue at Judge.

"All right, Thomas, let's get riding," he said. "We're expected down on the river and not a moment too soon. They're going to start sending the boys down the James as soon as Comte de Grasse gets the British Navy under control. If he does," he added under his breath.

Doesn't Papa have any faith about anything? Thomas thought as the horses picked through a huge puddle and made their way toward the river. *He doubts our winning the war. He doesn't think Sam is coming back.* Thomas kept his eyes on the soldiers they passed. *Funny. Papa's the one who taught* me *about faith.*

"Thomas!" Papa said sharply.

Thomas jumped in time to see a tree branch looming

ahead. He ducked before it could slap him in the face.

"You've seen military camps before," his father said. "Look ahead now or you'll have your head lopped off."

Thomas nodded obediently and faced forward. But he couldn't keep his eyes from cutting to the side, for just one glimpse of Sam.

Papa pulled Judge to a halt on the side of a horse path that ran along the river. Thomas looked around and hugged himself. It was spooky here, with murky Mill Creek ahead and the James River on one side of them and a deep hardwood glade on the other that looked as if it came from some dark legend.

Caroline would already have a pretend game spinning in her head for this place, Thomas thought.

"Mr. Hutchinson, sir!" an officer in a Virginia militia uniform sang out. He came toward them with his hand already outstretched to shake Papa's. "Those boats arrived from your shipyard in Yorktown in the middle of the night, though how the soldiers did it I'll never know. The place is lousy with British. But we certainly want to thank you—"

"No thanks necessary," Papa said. "I only want to help get our men to Yorktown to meet Cornwallis and get this whole thing over with." Papa dismounted and stretched. "Where are the vessels? I'd like to inspect them."

Thomas wrapped Burgess's reins loosely around a branch and followed as the officer led them down to the river. Across from a narrow channel of the James was the island of Jamestown, still looking asleep. Thomas shivered. A lot of people had died on that island when the British had first tried to establish a colony in Virginia. It seemed like thoughts of death were all around. And Thomas didn't like having them.

When they reached the marshy edge of the James, the

officer picked his way among the bulrushes and pulled a row of them back. There, nestled in hiding among them, was a brand new barge.

"One of three," the officer said.

"They will take only a fraction of your men, I know," Papa said. "I wish I could do more."

"You've done more than you know, Mr. Hutchinson," the officer said. "News of your generosity has spread, and other planters are donating equipment and supplies."

As their conversation went on, Thomas backed carefully away from the bank. Although the air was warming up, he still felt a chill going up his spine.

It's this creepy place, Thomas thought as he swept another nervous glance at Jamestown Island. *It's as if all those dead colonists are still there, watching me.*

He shook his head to get the ghostly thoughts out of it. But even as he did, something caught his eye . . . across the little finger of the river . . . on the shore of Jamestown Island. He stopped and stared.

Something had moved over there.

There's no one on that part of Jamestown Island now, ninny, Thomas scolded himself. *It was probably nothing but a raccoon scavenging.*

But he kept his gaze glued to the spot on the shore. As he watched, the scrub pines at the river's edge shook as if something had grabbed hold of them and was about to push them apart.

Something is looking back at me! Thomas thought with a start. *Maybe it's just deer, like yesterday.*

But there was a hand—no, two hands—pressing against the pine needles. And a face peeking between the branches.

Without knowing why, Thomas ducked into the tall grass. Peeking between the stalks, he saw a person's head poke cautiously out.

Thomas gasped out loud. It wasn't just any person's head. It was a blond head with a square jaw, attached to a pair of broad shoulders. Hutchinson shoulders.

It was his brother Sam.

Thomas lurched from the grass with a cry, and the scrub pines sprang back into place. Jamestown Island was empty again.

Thomas scrambled up and sloshed to the riverbank, sinking in up to his ankles.

"Sam!" he called. "It's me—Thomas! Sam!"

There was no answer from the opposite shore.

"Sam!" Thomas screamed. He splashed forward until he was in up to his knees. "Sam Hutchinson! It's all right! It's your brother! It's Thomas!"

"Thomas."

A heavy hand came down on his shoulder, and he whirled around. Papa's eyes bore into his.

"Thomas, what are you doing?" his father said.

"I saw Sam!" Thomas cried. "He was over there on the island, looking through those pines—"

"No, he wasn't, son," Papa said.

"But I *saw* him."

"Sir, is there something I can help with?" the militiaman said from behind them.

"No," John Hutchinson said. "My son thinks he saw his brother across the way, on the island."

"He's a soldier, is he?" the officer said.

"Yes!" Thomas said, jabbing his pointing finger out so

frantically that he sent up a spray of river water. "He was right over there."

The officer cleared his throat. "I'm afraid you didn't see him there. The only soldiers camped on Jamestown Island are on the other side, across Sandy Bay at the Towne. Any soldier on this side would probably be a deserter!"

There was a stunned silence, and the officer's face flushed scarlet. "Sir," he stammered, "I did not mean to suggest—"

"No offense taken," Papa said. He squeezed Thomas's shoulder. "Whether there was a soldier there or not, deserter or no, it was not my son."

"But it *was,* Papa! I *saw*—"

"Thomas, enough!"

The words stabbed into Thomas, and he cringed as The Look formed on his father's face. The officer ducked his head and moved away.

"Thomas, I have had men contact the military camp at Jamestown as recently as yesterday," Papa said. "Your brother is not there."

The Look was piercing into Thomas like a blade, but for the first time in his life, Thomas didn't care. *Let Papa look at me all he wants,* he thought angrily, *but Sam is coming home.*

Papa was still holding Thomas's shoulder, and he shook it now, almost roughly. "I have not told this to your mother, and I won't until I'm absolutely certain. I wasn't going to tell you, but you force me to." John Hutchinson sighed. "I spoke to one of General Washington's aides yesterday, on the distant possibility that Samuel might have been with some of the northern troops—"

"But Sam was with Nathaniel Greene!" Thomas cried. "He's probably gone back to Carolina—"

"Listen to me. The aide said they'd had several young men join them after Greene left Virginia. I showed him the miniature I always carry of Samuel." Papa drew a long breath. "He said he was sure he'd seen him . . . piled with some other soldiers on the back of a wagon."

"It isn't true!"

"No more!" The words roared out of his father. Papa took him by both shoulders with his beefy hands and yanked Thomas up close to his face. "Believe your foolishness if you will, son," he said with his blue eyes blazing, "but I'll hear no more such talk. I know that I am asking you to become a man before your time, but these are desperate times that call for growing up too fast. There is no time for clinging to useless hopes."

Thomas opened his mouth.

"No, Thomas," his father said tightly. "Do not speak of this. Do not speak of it again."

Thomas wrenched himself away and ran—blindly, with branches slapping his face and his feet stumbling into holes and over rocks. His heart thundered in his chest, and the thoughts thundered through his head.

He's wrong! Papa's wrong! Sam is alive!

His breathing began to wheeze, and Thomas slowed to a walk and clutched at his aching side. His thoughts slowed down, too, and a new one fell into step with the others. *"Any soldier on this side would probably be a deserter,"* that officer had said.

"No!" Thomas cried out to the live oaks that bordered the road. "Not Sam!"

And then he hung his head and started to cry. He stopped only when Judge clopped up beside him, with

Burgess's hoofbeats close behind.

"Get on, Thomas," his father said quietly.

Thomas wiped his sleeve across his eyes and climbed onto Burgess's back.

"Put this in your money pouch," Papa said.

Thomas looked woodenly at the object his father was tucking into his hand. He turned it over and saw Sam's painted face looking at him from out of a small oval. It was the same face he'd seen across the river, on the island. He knew it.

"Thank you, sir," he murmured. Then he put the miniature into his pouch and they rode back to Williamsburg without saying another word.

✢ ✤ ✢

hen Thomas reported for work at the apothecary shop that afternoon, he was in no mood to talk to anyone.

There was a prickly feeling at the back of his neck, like the one he used to get a lot, back in the days when he would just as soon have blackened a fellow's eye as look at him. He hadn't felt that in a long time, but it was there now, and he was bristling with it as he pushed open the side door into the back hall of Francis's shop. The feeling turned up to a sizzle when he started into the main shop and saw who was standing at the counter.

"Come on, Pickering, step on it!" Winifred was saying in her no-nonsense voice. "I have patients waiting for their medicine!"

"All you had to do was send word," Francis grumbled as he dumped a handful of licorice root and sugar drops into a jar.

"Send word how? A passing pigeon?" she said crisply. "There's no one there but Nicholas and me. Where's that black-haired boy, that child Nicholas is always raving about?"

Thomas slipped back into the hallway and flattened himself against the wall.

"You're talking about young Hutchinson," Francis said.

"Whatever his name is, where is he? Why hasn't he reported for duty today?"

"He works for me, not you."

"Hmmm," Winifred said.

What does hmmm mean? Thomas wondered. *She always says that.*

"Will there be anything else?" he heard Francis grumble.

"Not now, but there may be later. I'm going to have to find myself a messenger."

Francis just grunted.

"If you run out of things for that boy to do here, send him to the hospital. He's at least strong if nothing else."

If nothing else? Thomas thought, bristling. But his thoughts were cut off by the sound of footsteps coming closer.

"You may use the front door," Francis said.

"I'm not a customer," said Winifred. "I'm just the help."

And before Thomas could move, she was in the hallway with him, headed for the side door. The indignant expression was still on his face when she skidded to a halt and stared at him.

"Listening in the shadows, were you?" she said.

I'll listen anywhere I please, Thomas wanted to say to her.

"That's probably the only way you'll ever get any information around here," she said briskly. She shifted her basket of packages onto her other arm and straightened her shoulders. Thomas realized for the first time that she was wearing a dress, though it was gray and plain.

"What are you looking at?" Winifred said. She shook her head so that the long, red braid swung across her back. "You are the staringest boy I've ever seen. If you want to stare, come stare at the hospital when you're finished here."

And she was gone, as if she'd never get where she was going if she didn't go at full tilt.

Who does she think she is, giving me orders? Thomas thought. *Francis will never stand for that.*

He swung around the corner to find Francis bent over his mortar and pestle, grinding up rattlesnake root.

"She surely thinks she's something, doesn't she, sir?" Thomas said.

Francis gave a grunt and flipped his eyes up over his spectacles. "Whether she is or not, she's all we've got," he said.

Thomas picked up the broom and began to sweep the pine floorboards. "You like her, then?"

"It isn't a matter of liking her," Francis said in his wheezy voice. He stopped to cough. "She gets the job done."

Thomas pushed some dirt toward the door, but he kept his eyes on Mr. Pickering. "Then you don't mind taking orders from *her?*"

"She can give all the orders she wants—that's just her way. I'll do as I choose."

Thomas grinned with relief.

"As soon as you finish sweeping up, I want you to take this over to the hospital for that Frenchman's fever. And then stay there and help out. I won't need you here for a while."

Thomas nearly dropped the broom. "I'm to go over there . . . and work with *her?*"

"Don't worry, Hutchinson," Francis said snappishly. "It will count same as your time here."

"I don't want to work for her!"

"Then you don't want to work for me either," Francis said in a voice as dry as dust. "Like it or not, we're all in this war together."

Numbly, Thomas stared.

"Don't start sulking, Hutchinson, or you'll be out of a job," Francis said. "Do what she says, just like you do for me."

She's not like you, Thomas thought stubbornly. But he dragged his feet back to the counter.

"You'd think I was sending you into battle," Francis said as he put the container of rattlesnake root into Thomas's hand. "She's a harmless woman. She isn't going to bite you."

Don't count on it, Thomas thought miserably.

As it turned out, every word she spoke to Thomas that afternoon chewed into him as if he were a bone some dog was gnawing on.

"Look alive, sonny, there's three more patients who need water and hard tack. . . . Sweeping isn't going to keep this place clean, sonny. Get some rags and wash water and go after that floor. . . . Come over here, sonny, and I'll show you how to wrap a patient who has fever."

"I already know how," Thomas told her. "Nicholas taught me."

She cocked one of her auburn eyebrows at him. "Then you've learned from the best."

"And my name isn't sonny."

She waved him off and bustled toward the Frenchman's bed. "I know, it's Timothy or some such—"

"Thomas."

"Fine, fine. Now let's get this patient wrapped, sonny."

"All right, missy," Thomas mumbled. His backbone was prickling like he had poison ivy.

"Good afternoon, Louis," Winifred said to the Frenchman, in the softened version of her voice Thomas had only heard her use with the patients.

Louis smiled wanly out of his tangled beard and reached up a hand to touch hers.

"Ah, angel," Louis said in his stilted English.

Thomas rolled his eyes.

"Now, Louis, I know you're burning up with fever and the last thing you want is to be kept warm, but you must trust that we know what we're doing."

"Oui, mademoiselle."

"Please," she said, "my friends call me Winnie."

"But you may call her Winifred or *Mistress* deWindt," whined a voice from the next bed. Xavier flopped his wobbly body restlessly and peered at them out of his poke-hole eyes.

"No," said Winifred. *"You* may call me Mistress deWindt. Louis may call me Winnie. All right, sonny, help me roll Louis over so we can get these blankets around him."

"I am an officer in the Virginia militia!" Xavier bellowed.

"Congratulations, Jowls," Winifred said dryly. "That's good, sonny, now wrap that nice and tight . . . that's it."

Xavier sniffed and said, "My men do not treat me with this utter disrespect, and I'll not have it from you!"

"Then get up off of your flabby backside and go back to your men where you belong." Winifred never looked at him. She just kept wrapping the blankets around Louis, with her nut-hard face gleaming like an acorn.

Thomas handed her another blanket. *At least that's one good thing about her,* he thought. *She knows how to put*

Xavier Wormeley in his place.

"Tighter, sonny. We'll never sweat it out of him the way you're doing it."

But that's the only thing good about her, he added to himself. He gave the blanket a tug.

"There," he said. "Is that good enough?"

She flashed her eyes briskly over the blanket and nodded like a sparrow. "It'll do. Now, where is that rattlesnake root you brought?"

Thomas hurried toward the medicine cabinet. Nicholas was just closing it when he got there, and he smiled his quivering smile down at Thomas.

"It's good to have you working with us, Thomas," he said.

Thomas twisted his mouth. *I wish I was working with you,* he thought. *But I'm only working with* her!

"I know you've learned a great deal from me, but there is more you can learn from Winnie," the doctor went on. "I've learned new techniques from her already these last two days. And to think I was about to send her home."

Nicholas drifted away, eyes glazed over as he watched Winnie at her work. Thomas looked at him in disgust.

"What's the matter, lad?" said a voice at his elbow. "Do you smell somethin' bad?"

Thomas turned to see Malcolm leaning jauntily against the medicine cabinet.

"Why did you sneak up on me?" Thomas asked.

Malcolm grinned his square grin. "I think my sneakin' up on you is the least of your worries. You've got Xavier the Worm snarlin' at you and Winnie the Wonder Nurse barkin' at you and Nicholas the Nipped-by-Love wanderin' around in a smitten state. It's a wonder he doesn't run into somethin' and hurt himself. Keep an eye on him, lad."

Malcolm chuckled, and Thomas gave him a poke in the stomach.

"It isn't funny," Thomas said. "I'm stuck here, taking orders from her. Francis sent me!"

"*Esther* sent me," Malcolm said. He produced a large basket from which several loaves of bread stuck out. "And then I'm on my way. Too bad you can't do the same."

"Shut it," Thomas said miserably.

"Sonny! Over here!" Winifred called from Louis's pallet.

"Your mistress calls," Malcolm whispered to him.

Thomas dragged himself over to Louis, and he could feel Malcolm bobbing mischievously along behind him. Beads of sweat dotted the Frenchman's forehead, and several had trickled down his face and into his beard.

"Louis here and I were discussing it, and we both think he would feel so much better if his face were shaved," Winifred said. "I'd do it, but I haven't the time. Get a razor and some soap and water, sonny, and take that beard off."

"Me?" Thomas cried. "I never shaved anyone in my life!"

Winifred peered closely at him as if she were seeing him for the first time. "Oh, you aren't old enough, are you? You look like you ought to be." Her eyes darted busily over Thomas's shoulder and landed on Malcolm. "What about you, then?"

Thomas twisted to look at Malcolm. The servant boy looked startled.

"Yes. What about me?" Malcolm said.

"You shave him," she said. "You've obviously done it before."

Thomas squinted at Malcolm's chin. "You have?"

"So find us a razor and go to work," Winifred said.

"I beg your pardon," Malcolm said stiffly. "I do shave—"

"You *do?*" Thomas said.

"—but I work for John Hutchinson, and I do not have time—"

"I'm sure His Majesty can spare you for the time it will take to give Louis some relief."

And then as if the matter were settled, she dusted off her hands and bustled toward a pallet on the other side of the ballroom.

"Now see here!" Malcolm called after her.

"What did she mean 'His Majesty'?" Thomas asked. "And when did you start shaving, Malcolm?"

"Who is she thinkin' she is?" Malcolm said darkly.

"Monsieur?" said a soft voice below them.

They both looked down at Louis, whose sweaty face was turned gratefully toward them. He pointed to a leather bag on the chair next to his pallet, and Thomas peeked into it. He pulled out a razor.

Malcolm sighed. "Get some soap and water, lad."

By the time Malcolm had rendered Louis's face clean and smooth, two other soldiers were calling weakly from their beds that they would like a shave as well.

"I'm not a barber," Malcolm grumbled at first. "Esther and Otis are going to have my hide if I don't get back."

Winifred couldn't have heard him from where she was spooning soup into another man's mouth, but she snapped out, "You have time for a few more, there, Scottie. What's more important than our fighting men?"

Malcolm gave a grudging grunt. "She's right there," he muttered to Thomas. "And that's the only reason I'm stayin'."

Malcolm stayed until nearly dark, shaving one man after

another until everyone except Xavier Wormeley had a smooth face. The jowled man turned his back on the whole scene and slept all afternoon.

Only the dwindling light of late afternoon was left in the sky as Malcolm and Thomas made their way down the Palace Green toward the Hutchinsons' house. Although it was still September, a few leaves were starting to yellow. It was the time of year for storms, and the gathering winds of a new one were sending leaves to the ground. Thomas picked one up as they walked. With the hospital and Winifred fading behind them, his thoughts turned back to what had happened at Jamestown, and he told Malcolm about it.

When they reached the Hutchinsons' garden gate, Malcolm stopped and put his hand on the gate post. The wind whipped through his shaggy black hair, and to Thomas's surprise, his dark eyes looked stormy, too.

"So Sam's alive and still fightin', eh?" Malcolm said.

"*You* believe me, then?" Thomas said.

"Of course I believe you, lad. You saw him, didn't you? What I'm thinkin' is that if they have soldiers even out on Jamestown Island, this truly is going to be an all-out battle." He clutched the gate. "I'd give anything to be out there fightin' it with them."

"Why?" Thomas said anxiously.

Malcolm's cloudy eyes passed over the Hutchinsons' yard, where a hen flapped her way under the porch and squawked for her brood of chicks to come and join her, out of the wind. But Thomas knew he wasn't watching them at all. His eyes were on some distant battlefield. The thought seized Thomas like a strangling hand.

"Because they're fightin' this war for people like me, lad,"

Malcolm said finally. "They're fightin' for freedom so that if I want to do somethin' with my life besides work dawn to midnight takin' care of someone else's place, I can. Why wouldn't I want to be out there fightin' for it, too?"

The wind slapped a gust into Thomas's face, splattering it with the rain that was starting to fall. Thomas hardly noticed. Malcolm's words were hitting him harder than the storm.

"You can't," Thomas said flatly. "You have to be 16."

"Malcolm!" a voice called from the back steps of the house. Esther was flapping her skirt like hen's wings. "Don't you have sense enough to come in out of the rain? Get the firewood. We've company a-comin' for dinner!"

Malcolm looked at Thomas through the drops that poured between them. "You see what I mean? I have people like Esther decidin' for me all the time—like that biddy there decidin' her chicks need to be under the porch." He shook his shaggy-haired head. "I want to fight for the right to decide for myself."

"Malcolm!" Esther trumpeted across the yard. "Dr. Quincy and his lady friend will be here before you've got the fire laid! Come on, then!"

Malcolm and Thomas stared at each other.

"Dr. Quincy?" Malcolm said.

"And his lady friend?" Thomas said.

"Oh, no!" they said together.

And Thomas added one more, "Oh, no!"

✝ ✦ ✝

Chapter Seven

"Thomas, more venison?" Mama glanced at Thomas's plate, and her gray eyes clouded. "Why, you haven't even eaten your first helping!" She reached for his forehead. "Are you ill, son?"

At the other end of the table, Papa gave his company-at-the-table laugh. "That would be the only reason for Thomas not eating!" he said. "Nicholas, quickly, examine him!"

Across the table, Nicholas smiled politely. But the pale-blue eyes that met Thomas's weren't merry.

"I'm fine," Thomas said stiffly.

Quiet settled over the table again, the way it had several times since they'd sat down to dinner. Papa had made courteous conversation about the storm and the price of wheat, but they kept falling back into silence.

Winifred seemed to be casting most of the quiet-spell over the table. Mama had tried to chat with her, but Winifred gave only short yes and no answers and then folded and unfolded her hands in her lap.

I guess she can't talk at all if she can't bark orders at people, Thomas thought.

Papa stirred. "Let me ask you this, Nicholas. How can I make it easier, what with the battle about to begin so close by?"

Nicholas shifted in his seat. Winifred looked into her lap. Mama and Papa exchanged questioning glances. Thomas pulled himself out of his own sulking thoughts and looked around the table.

What is going on here? he thought.

Nicholas breathed into his hands. "You can be a great deal of help, actually, John," he said. Nicholas tried to look at Winnie, but she wouldn't look back. "What I am hearing is true, is it not? The fighting is going to begin very soon in Yorktown?"

Papa nodded. "It is. When Thomas and I returned from the river today, I learned that early this morning, Comte de Grasse sent the British Navy into retreat on the Chesapeake Bay. Washington will leave for Yorktown in the next few days."

"What does that mean, John?" Virginia Hutchinson said.

"It means that not only do the French have Cornwallis blocked off by sea, but they have made way for another French convoy from the north to get through with more supplies for our men and more weapons and ammunition."

"That's good news," Mama said.

"I am not happy that a battle is about to begin," Papa said. "I hate to think of men losing their lives. But at least it will be over with soon." He looked curiously at Nicholas. "Why this sudden interest in the war, Doctor? I thought you wanted no part of it as a Quaker."

"I have no interest in war," Nicholas said. He glanced

anxiously at Winnie's bowed head. "But I am interested in saving lives."

She still didn't look up, and Nicholas's mouth trembled as he looked back at Papa. "I am going to the battlefront to doctor the soldiers there."

Thomas felt his heart skip a beat. He stared at Nicholas and then at his father and then at his mother. When his eyes stopped on Winifred, he saw that her shoulders were sagging.

"Good heavens, Nicholas," Papa said quietly. "Do you know what kind of risk you're taking—with your own life?"

"No more than any of those men and boys are taking with theirs," Nicholas said.

There was another silence, one Thomas couldn't stand.

"I don't understand!" he burst out. "Last spring when Mr. Wormeley tried to force you to go to the battle, you went to jail instead!"

Winifred's head bobbed up, and Thomas saw that her face was blotchy red. Nicholas looked at her as if *she* had asked the question, not Thomas.

"Xavier Wormeley wanted me to join the army and work as part of the military unit. That meant I would be part of the war, and I couldn't do that. Not in good conscience. But this I am doing on my own, because God wills it. I am not part of the war—I am part of the cure. It is the same as my running a hospital here."

"No, it isn't!" Winifred said, her voice raspy. "Here, you will not be hit by flying musket shot and cannonballs!"

"Here, I cannot get to the men before they bleed to death," Nicholas said quietly.

Thomas's heart started beating again, deep in the pit of his chest. There was no use arguing with Nicholas now. He looked calm again, as if he were in charge, the way he did when they walked into a sick person's room. Thomas put his fork down and leaned heavily back in his chair.

Mama looked at Winifred with sad eyes. "Will you be going back to Pennsylvania, then?"

Winifred flapped her braid as she shook her head.

"Winnie insists on staying to run the hospital while I go to Yorktown," Nicholas said.

Thomas felt his mouth falling open.

"She's not strong—" Nicholas started to say.

"Nicholas, please," Winifred said through clenched teeth.

Nicholas bit his lip and started over. "I can leave the hospital in no more capable hands."

Thomas snatched up his tankard and drank to keep from yelping. Nicholas's eyes swam and Winifred clasped and unclasped her hands a dozen times and soon everyone at the table seemed to be on the verge of tears. Thomas was on the verge of punching something.

Finally, Papa broke the awkward silence. "Well, then, Nicholas, what can I do for you—and for the hospital—to ensure the success of this mission of yours?"

Nicholas looked at Winifred, who stopped folding her hands.

"I need more help at the hospital, sir," she said.

"Please, call me John," Papa said.

How about "His Majesty"? Thomas thought bitterly.

"The ladies can provide more food and bandages and bed linens," Mama said.

"I would appreciate that," Winifred said. She turned her head crisply toward Papa, and Thomas gave a silent groan. The real Winifred was coming back. "But what I truly need are more hands. Francis Pickering has generously given me more of his time, and his boy here, too." She nodded at Thomas. "But with wounded coming in, that isn't going to be enough, now that I have to do Nicholas's work, too."

"Can anyone be taught?" Mama asked.

"Anyone with two hands," Winifred said in her brisk way.

Mama studied her delicate pink palms and nodded. "Then I am at your service, Mistress deWindt, and I'm sure I can speak for Lydia Clark and some of the other women as well. Esther can take care of things here."

Thomas could only stare, open-mouthed, as Winifred squeezed Mama's hand.

"What else?" Papa said.

The dining room door opened and Malcolm came in with a tray full of sponge cake and fruit. He set it on a side table and began to clear away the dinner dishes. Thomas glared at him until he looked. *Pay attention to this conversation,* he said with his eyes. Malcolm went on piling up the chargers and porringers as if he could have cared less what was going on, but Thomas knew he was now listening to every word.

"As Nicholas said, there are some things I simply cannot do," Winifred said. "Turning the patients in their beds, for instance. And some of the men object to being bathed by a woman." She glanced at Thomas. "Sonny here is a big help, but I need at least one more man."

"Most of the men and boys have either gone off to the war or they have important jobs here already," Mama said. "I don't know who—"

"I do," Papa said.

He was leaning back in his side chair with his hands folded on his chest, watching someone carefully. Thomas followed his gaze . . . to Malcolm.

"Scottie here?" Winifred asked. Her eyes lit up like candle flames.

"We like to call him Malcolm," Papa said, grinning. "Malcolm, can you be spared around here for several hours a day?"

Malcolm's black eyes were wild. "I, uh . . . I don't think so, sir. Not with all the wood to be chopped and the horses to be dealt with—"

"Thomas can help you. I think it's time we got you out of that kitchen anyway. You can make a contribution to the war you're so interested in."

Thomas knew Papa wanted Malcolm to like the idea. Thomas could see that Malcolm didn't.

But the servant boy nodded his shaggy head and said, "Whatever you think is best, sir."

"Good, then," Papa said. "Mistress deWindt, it looks as if you have yourself a company."

Winifred didn't smile, but her face was nut-shiny as she looked around the table. "We start tomorrow, then," she said briskly. "And I beg your pardon, Mistress Hutchinson, but you will want to leave your ruffles at home."

Mama's eyes sparkled and she gave a smart little salute.

Thomas held back a growl. *Now she's telling Mama how to dress. Next thing you know she'll be telling us all what to eat.*

"Sponge cake, Winifred?" Mama offered.

"I never touch it," Winifred said. "Too much sugar is bad for you, you know."

"Oh," Mama said, "then I'll pass it up, too."

Thomas scowled and took two pieces.

Nicholas and Winifred finally left after the fruit and nuts were finished. Thomas couldn't have been in a fouler mood as he gave a stiff good-bye wave from the doorway and stomped off toward the stairs and the safety of his room.

"Thomas," his father said behind him, "I would like to speak with you in the library."

No! No more today, please! Thomas screamed inside himself. But he plodded into his father's library in the back hall without a word.

Papa settled himself behind his desk and motioned for Thomas to sit in the green-checked chair. The place smelled of Papa—leather, sweat, and licorice. Papa offered Thomas a dish of licorice drops, but Thomas shook his head.

Papa watched him as he slowly put the dish down. "I see you're unhappy, son."

Thomas shrugged.

"I'm sure it has mostly to do with your brother Sam. I understand that, Thomas, and I'm sorry I was so harsh with you about it."

"It's all right, sir," Thomas lied. It wasn't all right at all. Not as long as Papa refused to believe that Sam was still alive.

"So much is changing and so rapidly, I would be concerned if you *weren't* affected by it." Papa picked up a piece of paper. "I want to read you part of Clayton's letter." The back of Thomas's neck bristled as Papa began to read aloud.

I wondered many times after I left you in Yorktown if I was indeed doing the right thing by coming to England. I was green with seasickness on the ship (I will never be the sailor Great-Grandfather Josiah Hutchinson was), and I was greeted with hostile stares when I disembarked in London. Even when I was presented to the bishop for examination before my ordination, I felt as if I were on trial for murder. Why, I wondered, am I here?

And why, I wonder, is Papa reading this to me? Thomas thought. He squirmed miserably on the chair. Papa continued reading.

But Father, when I was down on my knees at the altar, presenting myself to be God's servant forever, I thought I felt hands on my head. I was not warned beforehand that the bishop would be laying hands on me, and I looked up in surprise. But no one was touching me. All eyes were closed in prayer, all hands folded. The hands I felt on me, Father, were God's own. I knew that no matter what I had to endure to come here, God's hand was in it. I am doing His will.

It was quiet in the room except for the rustling of parchment as Thomas's father folded the letter.

Thomas clenched his hands on his knees and thought, *Well? What I supposed to say now?*

"Clayton," Papa said finally, "has felt God's hand in his life. I think we all can if we are willing to get quiet and pay attention." He looked hard at Thomas. "That is what I am trying to do as we move forward through these last difficult days of the war. I encourage you to do the same."

Thomas squeezed his hands harder.

"Let it be, Thomas," his father said. "And then listen. You'll feel God's hand, just as Clayton has. Just as Nicholas has."

Just as Sam has? Thomas wanted to cry. Instead, he stood up, hands still clenched at his sides. "Will that be all, sir?" he said.

For a moment, it looked as if there might be more. But then Papa shook his head and nodded for Thomas to go.

Thomas couldn't get out of the library and up the stairs to his room fast enough. He slammed the door behind him and went to the window, where outside the storm was raging just like the one going on inside him.

God? Thomas prayed the way he always did at the window. But nothing else would come—except anger.

And as he gnawed at the inside of his mouth he realized there was almost no one he *wasn't* angry with right now, including God.

The only people I'm not mad at are Caroline and Patsy and Malcolm, he thought. *Those are the only people I can depend on anymore.*

He unfastened the money belt to get ready for bed. It fell to the floor with a thud, and Thomas remembered the miniature of Sam his father had given him. He pulled open the bag and stared at his brother's face.

And you, Sam, he thought. *I can still depend on you.*

✛ ✚ ✛

Chapter Eight

Thomas looked up sleepily from his pillow the next morning as Malcolm burst in and yanked off Thomas's quilts.

"Hey!" Thomas cried.

"Get up. The storm's over and you're to come help me with the chores so we can go to the hospital."

Thomas snatched up the covers again. "I don't go there until afternoon!"

"Not anymore."

"Says who?"

"Says Major deWindbag." Malcolm gave the woodpile a kick.

"What are you going to do?" Thomas asked.

"About what?"

"About the Windbag?"

"What I always do—as I'm told."

Thomas watched him. This was not his happy-go-lucky Malcolm. This was an angry Malcolm who was about to pick up a piece of firewood and hurl it through the window. It suddenly felt good to have someone to be angry with. Thomas scrambled out of bed.

"Maybe this is a job for the Fearsome Foursome," Thomas said.

"What are you talking about?" Malcolm said irritably. "Come on, Thomas, we have work to do."

"No!" Thomas said. "Perhaps you and Patsy and Caroline and I can make it so miserable for Winifred that she won't want to stay and—"

"And the soldiers will be left with no one to take care of them. Excellent idea, Thomas, but from now on would you be keepin' those brilliant thoughts to yourself? I have enough to worry about."

Thomas stared at him.

"I mean it, lad," Malcolm said as he headed for the door. "I've no time for foolish games anymore. Now get dressed. We've grain to take to the mill."

Thomas watched the door close and felt the hair on the back of his neck stand up in protest. *All right,* he thought angrily. *So perhaps Patsy and Caroline are the only people I'm not mad at!*

Malcolm had Burgess hitched up when Thomas got downstairs. The wagon was loaded with wheat Papa had brought from the plantation to be taken to Caroline's father's mill and ground into flour.

Thomas hopped sulkily onto the wagon and folded his arms.

"What are you poutin' for, lad?" Malcolm said as he coaxed Burgess out into the puddles on the street.

Thomas shrugged.

"I didn't mean to offend you, lad," Malcolm said. "I just have a good deal on my mind now."

"Leave me alone, Malcolm," Thomas said.

Malcolm did.

They didn't speak until they reached the mill, and Malcolm said, "Would you look at that!"

Thomas looked—and gasped.

The four rectangular sails of Robert Taylor's mill could always be seen spinning in the wind from all over Williamsburg. But today, the wheel of sails was deathly still, and two of its frames were naked. The cloth that covered them had been stripped away and what was left was hanging in rags.

On the ground below, slender Robert Taylor was hurrying about, shouting things to a man who was hitching two oxen to the mill.

"Give it one turn and we'll have the broken sail down here where we can work on it!" Thomas heard Mr. Taylor call out. His face, always serious, was even more somber than ever.

"What happened?" Thomas asked Malcolm.

"Looks like the wind grabbed it during the storm," Malcolm said. "Robert Taylor is lucky the whole thing didn't go over."

"Lucky, eh?"

Malcolm and Thomas both turned to look at the man who had spoken from a wagon near theirs. Thomas saw that it was George Fenton, the gunsmith.

He spat over the side of his wagon. "It wouldn't bother me if the thing burned down. It could, you know, if he used the brake during a strong wind—the friction would set up a spark that would take the whole mill down. And it wouldn't bother me a bit. I go all the way out to the Digges's plantation and use their mill now."

"Why?" Thomas said.

"Because Taylor's a lousy Loyalist, that's why!"

"I never knew you felt that way, Mr. Fenton," Malcolm said.

"I kept my mouth shut before. Who knew how the war was going to turn out? But now I think we ought to run him out of town—or worse." Fenton narrowed his eyes at Thomas. "And you can tell your Loyalist-sympathizing father I said that."

"My father is just protecting their rights like he's supposed to," Thomas said.

Fenton spat once more. "As far as I'm concerned, they don't have any rights anymore." He clicked his tongue at his horse and started off. "Hey, Taylor!" he yelled as he pulled off through the puddles. "I hope it burns to the ground next time!"

Thomas looked quickly at the mill. Caroline was standing next to the oxen's heads, petting their noses, and her brown eyes followed George Fenton all the way to the end of North England Street.

Thomas scrambled down from the wagon and ran to her. She tried to lift her chin when she saw him, but he could tell her eyes were prickling with hurt.

"He's a hateful old windbag!" Thomas said.

"I didn't pay any attention to him," Caroline said. She tossed her blonde hair back over her shoulders.

"How can you say that? I'll tell my Papa—he'll get after George Fenton for that!"

Caroline shook her head, and the lace on her pale yellow mob cap bobbed around her face. "My papa says I'm supposed to ignore it."

"Taylor!" another voice called from North England Street. "It's God's punishment for bein' a Loyalist!"

Thomas looked quickly at Caroline. She was petting the oxen so hard that he was surprised she didn't draw blood. Tears sparkled in her brown eyes.

"How can you ignore *that?*" Thomas said. "It isn't right!"

"It will burn next time!" someone else cried from their wagon. "And I hope you with it!"

Thomas heard Caroline gasp.

Anger sizzled up his backbone like a wildfire. He let go of the oxen and tore for the road.

"Thomas!" he heard Malcolm call out behind him. "What are you doin', lad?"

But Thomas careered through a puddle and threw himself up onto the wagon where the red-whiskered leather-smith was just opening his mouth to hurl another insult.

"What in the name of Beelzebub?" the leathersmith cried.

Thomas lunged at him with his fists flying. He felt one punch connect with the leathersmith's stomach before the man got to his feet and grabbed hold of Thomas's neck. Thomas choked, but he kept flailing and punching. The wagon lurched and there was another set of hands on him— wiry ones that tore him away and flung him down.

"Are you going to come after me, too?" the leathersmith shouted.

"No!" Malcolm said. "I'm gettin' him out of here before he hurts you!"

Red Whiskers gave a hard laugh, but he said, "Get him off my wagon!"

As soon as Malcolm had Thomas on the ground, the

leathersmith drove the wagon off down the street with his red hair flying.

"What were you thinkin' of, lad?" Malcolm said as he pulled Thomas to his feet.

"What difference does it make? She was crying!"

Malcolm shot up a bushy eyebrow. "So you had to try to break the man's neck?"

"Yes!" Thomas said stubbornly.

"No, Tom." Caroline stepped up beside him, hands on her tiny hips. "I hate fighting. You haven't done it in a long time."

Thomas stared at her, and he knew his face was burning, just the way his insides were. "I couldn't just stand there and let him yell those ugly things," he said.

"Why don't you take a walk, lad?" Malcolm said. "I'll take the wagon home. There will be no grindin' grain today anyway."

"No!" Thomas shouted at him.

"I don't care what you do, then," Malcolm said. "But you're not comin' near the wagon with that temper. You're likely to get us both killed."

Thomas kicked a stone and stomped off down North England Street, sending mud and rain water out in all directions from under his feet. But when he got to the corner of Nicholson Street, the fire inside was going out, and he dumped himself against Caroline's fence.

A moment later she was sitting beside him, pale yellow skirts billowing out around her over the mud. On the fence rail above them, Martha growled and then sprang down. Thomas watched warily as she gave him an indifferent hiss and then curled her fat orange self into Caroline's lap.

"You're not just mad about those people yelling, Tom,"

she said. "What's the matter?"

"Nothing."

"Liar."

Thomas sighed. Caroline was the only person who could call him "Tom" and "Liar" and even "Big, clumsy oaf" without making him mad. He stared down at his fingers and swallowed the lump in his throat.

"It's everything," he said.

He told her about seeing Sam, and about Papa not believing him and saying Sam was dead. Then he told her that Nicholas was going away to the battlefront, and that bossy Winifred was staying to run the hospital.

"She can't be that bad, can she?" Caroline said.

"Yes, she can—and she is."

Caroline jiggled the cat in her lap. "As bad as Martha?"

Martha opened one eye and stretched out a threatening claw.

"Yes," Thomas said stubbornly. "Pretty soon she'll be bossing the whole town. Mama and some of the ladies are going to be working there at the hospital, nursing the soldiers. Probably even Patsy, since Mistress Clark will be there. And Papa says Malcolm has to work for her part of the day, too. Everyone in town will be under her thumb!"

"Everyone but me," Caroline said. She scratched absently behind Martha's ears. All the dimples disappeared from her face.

"You're lucky, then," Thomas said. "This lady is—"

"Lucky?" Caroline cut in. "To be left out so that the only place we feel safe is in church? To be screamed at by the neighbors and told they hope my father dies?"

Thomas chewed his lip. "Well, no, but that's why I went after the leathersmith."

"Fighting isn't going to help, Tom."

"Then what is?"

She looked at him with a pale, pinched face. "Nothing is," she said. She hugged Martha to her until the cat grumbled. "It's different for people like Dr. Quincy. He can do something. I can't do anything."

Thomas looked at her, startled. "So you're not mad that he's going away?"

"Why should I be?"

"Because there's no one left!" Thomas cried. "Sam, Alexander, Clayton, and now Dr. Quincy! There's no one left but that cranky woman with hands like a man!"

He knew it sounded stupid, but he didn't care. He folded his arms heavily across his chest and pouted. There was a long silence. And then he heard a chuckle. He cut his eyes sideways to see Caroline grinning her slice-of-melon smile.

"Do you know how ridiculous you look, Tom?" she said.

"Yes. So don't start telling me."

She kept grinning. "Does she really have hands like a man?"

Thomas chewed at his lip, but he couldn't keep a smile from tugging at the corners of his mouth. "She does," he said.

Caroline giggled and poked him in the side with her elbow. "We still have you and me. We can still laugh. Isn't that something?"

Thomas shrugged and gave a half nod.

"It is and you know it," she said. "And no more fighting, Tom. No matter what happens."

Thomas shrugged again—and then he poked her back.

And when Martha gave a snarl and stretched herself awake, Thomas took off running with Caroline howling at his heels.

There wasn't much time in the next few days for fighting anyway—or much of anything except working. Each day started before dawn with Malcolm hauling Thomas out of bed to do chores before they left for the hospital.

Then Thomas's day went by in a blur of running from pallet to pallet, from ballroom to kitchen building, from Palace to apothecary shop. Everyone else seemed to be running, too.

Mama and the ladies were running up and down the aisles of pallets with pots of soup and tubs of bathwater. Francis was dashing from cellar to counter and back again trying to keep up with Winifred's demands for medicine. Even Winifred herself was running, following Nicholas around, getting instructions on the things she didn't already know before he left for Yorktown.

But Malcolm seemed to be moving faster than anyone, turning patients, hauling them from the wagons that brought them from the camps with their fevers and pneumonia. All the patients liked Malcolm, Thomas noticed—all except Xavier Wormeley who growled at Malcolm one day, "Why aren't you out fighting like the rest of the boys? You're a coward is why!" To Thomas's surprise, Malcolm just walked away from him and went on with his work.

Yet not enough was being accomplished for Winifred deWindt. She barked at them constantly, and complained that she had no messenger.

"She's a slave driver," Malcolm muttered to Thomas one afternoon as they leaned against the well drinking their first cup of water all day.

"She must be, because I feel like a slave," Thomas said.

Malcolm laughed in a superior say. "How would you know, lad? You've never been anyone's servant!"

"I am now! All I do is scrub floors and take orders! I haven't seen Caroline in three days."

Malcolm grinned.

"It isn't funny, Malcolm!"

"That isn't—but the fact that she is this minute spyin' on us from behind those rocks is pretty amusin' to me."

Thomas craned his neck to see behind the rocks in the garden a few feet away. Her head popped up, mob cap flouncing.

"How did you find me?" she said as she stomped over to them and set her basket on the ground.

"I told you," Malcolm said. "You and the lad here are easy to track! Besides," he added with a sniff, "I smelled that cat."

Caroline wrinkled her nose at him.

"What are you doing here?" Thomas asked, giving the basket a wide berth.

"I'm bored out of my mind," she said. "My papa would skin me alive if he knew, but I'm so lonely I just don't care."

"I guess he *wouldn't* be happy about your being at a Patriot hospital, lassie," Malcolm said. "Have you decided where you'll go?"

Caroline's brows puckered. "Go? What do you mean?"

"When the Patriots win the war, where will your family go?"

Caroline blinked at him.

Thomas glared and said, "Why do you say things like that, Malcolm?"

"Well, lad, when the war is over, it won't be safe for Loyalists to stay here. I'm surprised the Taylors have lasted this long, and they wouldn't have without your father's protection. Once the war's won, they won't have that anymore."

Thomas saw Caroline's face struggling, and he felt a sizzle of guilt. He was avoiding his father these days. He hadn't told him what those men had shouted at Robert Taylor that day at the mill. He turned and put his face close to Malcolm's.

"Shut it, Malcolm!" he said. "You don't know what you're talking about!"

"I beg your pardon, lad, but I do," Malcolm said. His voice was calm, but he didn't back away. "Don't get your dander up—"

"It's already up!" Thomas cried. "I want you to take back what you just said to Caroline. It's a lie. Take it back!"

"I won't," Malcolm said. His voice grew tighter. "And I'll not have you callin' me a liar."

"You *are* a liar! Now take it back!"

Before Malcolm could refuse again, Thomas gave Malcolm a shove.

"Don't!" Caroline screamed. "I'll let Martha out. So help me, I will!"

But Thomas gave Malcolm another shove, and Malcolm shoved him back—right into someone else's arms.

"Hold on, there, sonny," said Winifred deWindt. "There will be no fisticuffs at my hospital—unless it's with me."

✞ ⬧ ✞

Chapter Nine

homas pulled himself away, still breathing like an angry hog. He wanted to run, hard and fast, away from all of them. The only thing that kept him rooted to the spot were Winifred's crisp eyes.

"Quakers don't believe in fightin,'" Malcolm said to her.

"You're right, Scottie," she said. "But just because I don't believe in something doesn't mean I don't have the urge to do it sometimes. Isn't that right, sonny?"

Thomas looked at her in surprise, but then he stared down at the ground and shrugged. She was absolutely right. But she wasn't going to hear it from him.

"So," Winifred said, "you're the one who's keeping these boys from their work. And who might you be?"

Thomas did look up then to see Winnie surveying Caroline.

Caroline gave her slice-of-melon smile, exhibiting all two thousand dimples. "I'm Caroline Taylor. You must be Major deWindbag."

Thomas nearly choked. Beside him, he felt Malcolm

stiffen like a post. Winifred turned briskly and looked at both of them, face shining like an acorn. For a stunned moment, Thomas thought she was going to smile.

Instead she said, "I like that name. It gives me authority— and I'm sure I have the two of you to thank for it."

Winifred turned again to Caroline.

"So what are you doing just hanging about, missy?" she said. "There's work to be done, and you can do it. There's one younger than you in there carrying cups of soup and such."

"That would be Patsy," Caroline said brightly. "She's a friend of mine."

"Then she can tell you what to do." Winifred darted a glance over her shoulder at Malcolm and Thomas. "But mind you, it doesn't include dawdling with the likes of these. If you want to dawdle, do it with the soldiers—they could use some cheering up."

"All right, then!" Caroline said cheerfully, as if to prove she were just the person for the job.

"But you can't!" Thomas burst out.

"Why can't she?" Winifred said.

"Her father—"

"I can do anything I please," Caroline said. She was still smiling, but there were sparks firing from her brown eyes.

"Would it please you to be my messenger?" Winifred asked.

"What does that mean?" Caroline said.

"I need someone to run to the apothecary when we need more medicine, or to the ladies working at Mistress Wetherburn's to get more bandages—"

Her Papa will never let her do any of that! Thomas thought.

But Caroline bobbed her mob cap happily. "I can do that. I've lived in Williamsburg ever since I was born. I know where everything is."

"All right, then, missy, you're hired. Now, who's this Martha you were talking about? Is she someone who can help, too?"

"No!" Thomas and Malcolm said at the same time.

"She's my cat," Caroline said quickly.

"Oh," Winifred said. "Well, leave her at home, then." And with a brisk reminder to Malcolm and Thomas to get back to work, she disappeared into the hospital. Caroline was grinning as if she'd just won the entire war single-handedly.

"You're going to be in so much trouble with your father!" Thomas cried.

"Not if he doesn't know," she said, primly smoothing out her skirt.

"You're going to lie?"

"I'm just not going to tell." She shot them both a look. "And neither is anyone else."

"But why, lassie?" Malcolm said. "You're a Loyalist."

"Why do you have to keep reminding us, Malcolm?" Thomas said sourly.

"It doesn't matter," said Caroline. "Because I'm not doing it for Loyalists or Patriots. I'm doing it to show *you*, Malcolm Donaldson, that I am still going to be allowed to stay in Williamsburg no matter how the war turns out. Now I'm going to find Major deWindbag and get my orders."

"She'll be glad to give them to you," Thomas said dryly as she disappeared into the Palace.

"That's the least of her worries," Malcolm said. "Her father's a Loyalist, and that's all people will see."

Thomas felt the anger burning up his backbone again. "You don't know what you're talking about, Malcolm! And I'm tired of you talking about what's going to happen to Caroline's family and—"

"And scaring you?" Malcolm said.

"Sonny!" a voice barked from the door. "Do you think these men are going to get turned by themselves? Look lively now!"

Thomas glared at Malcolm and turned toward the Palace.

"Are you going to pout at the party tonight, too?"

Thomas turned to look at him.

"There's a going-away party for Nicholas tonight at the Raleigh Tavern," Malcolm said. "Everyone else is accepting the facts and making the best of them. I suggest you do the same."

"Shut it, Malcolm," Thomas said, and he stomped into the Palace.

Thomas felt more like there should be a funeral than a celebration. That evening as he, Mama, Papa, Esther, Otis, and Malcolm entered the tavern, his sour thoughts must have showed on his face.

Mama linked her arm through his and said, "That face is so much handsomer when it's smiling. What's troubling you?"

Thomas tugged miserably at the ribbons on his pale-blue waistcoat and shrugged.

Mama's gray eyes shone proudly. "If it's the suit you're worried about, dear, don't fret. You look every bit as handsome in it as Sam ever did."

"It isn't the suit!" Thomas snapped.

Mama's eyes looked stung, and at once Thomas caught The Look from his father.

Oh, no, he thought. *I'm in for it now.*

But Papa took Mama's arm. "It's been a long time since we've danced, my dear," he said. "Shall we?"

In the background Thomas could hear a minuet. He watched as Papa swept Mama into the Apollo Room. His chest felt pulled and tight.

It isn't the stupid suit, Thomas thought in anguish. *I just don't want any more people leaving!*

He squeezed his money pouch and closed his eyes. He could feel Sam's miniature inside, and he could imagine his brother's face looking back at him—from behind the scrub pines on Jamestown Island.

"What are you lollygaggin' around out here for, Hutchinson?" Francis Pickering said at his elbow. "The food's inside!"

Thomas followed him into the crowded room, which was twinkling with candles and lively with dancing and steeped in the aromas of pheasant, quail, apple tarts, and ginger cakes. Caroline skipped up to him with two silver cups of punch and put one in his hand.

"Isn't it wonderful, Tom?" she said. Her blonde hair was tied into a bunch of curls at the base of her neck, and she bounced them on purpose.

"How did you get those?" he said.

"You're not supposed to ask a girl her beauty secrets, Tom!"

"Huh?" Thomas said.

Caroline giggled and leaned close to his ear. "Mama does it with a metal rod she heats on the fire. It's quite frightening, really!"

Thomas sniffed. "It smells burnt."

Caroline laughed. "We actually did have to cut off one piece that got singed. Mama says she was curling her hair every day by the time she was my age, but she can't get me to sit still long enough."

Thomas looked down at Caroline, and he noticed that the ringlets touched her neck just right, and that her smile was prettier than anyone's in the room—

And then Thomas hugged his arms hard to his chest and frowned. *So?* he said roughly to himself. *What difference does it make that Caroline is pretty? Who cares?*

Just then a happy roar went up from the party crowd, and Caroline nudged Thomas.

"Look at Nicholas and Winifred dancing!" she cried.

Thomas felt his eyes bulging as he watched Nicholas stiffly walking the dance circle with Winifred's rough, red hand perched on his.

"You can tell they didn't take dancing lessons like we did," Caroline whispered to Thomas. She tugged at his sleeve. "Tom, you and I should dance!"

"No!" Thomas said.

"Why not?" She pulled playfully at a silver button on his coat. "We can't let all those lessons go to waste! Let's do!"

She put her little hand into his big, sweaty paw and gave it a tug. Thomas squeezed it back—and then felt a funny feeling in the pit of his stomach as if he didn't know what to do next.

This was Caroline. They'd been through all kinds of things together, including dancing lessons. But with her bouncy curls and her pink velvet dress and that lilac smell again, she was like a stranger to him.

He yanked his hand away. "No!" he said. "I don't want to dance with you!"

For a second, her brown eyes started open and flickered with hurt. And for that same second, Thomas was sorry.

But then she put her hands on her hips the way she had a hundred times before and said, "That's fine, Tom. Have a miserable time at the party—but do it with someone else."

And with one final flounce of her curls, she disappeared into the crowd of laughing people. Thomas had never felt less like laughing in his life. He hurried out of the room.

There seemed to be no one else out in the velvety end-of-September night as he crept out the door and perched tightly on the edge of one of the front steps. But as he tugged his knees to him and swallowed hard against the hurt in his throat, he saw two figures in the dark at the edge of the Duke of Gloucester Street. They were facing each other, holding both hands.

Thomas moaned silently. Nicholas and Winifred.

Making eyes at each other. Thomas shook his head. He wasn't sure what *making eyes* meant, but the sound of it made his stomach feel like he'd just eaten bad bacon.

Nicholas doesn't—I mean, it isn't like with Mama and Papa or something—

Thomas's thoughts trailed off as he watched Nicholas lean over and kiss Winnie on the cheek. Not awkwardly, like when he was dancing, but surely, like when he felt a sick person's forehead.

It's sick, all right, Thomas thought. *You won't catch me doing that.*

Of course, he added to himself as Nicholas let go of Winifred and she slipped off into the shadows, *I never thought I'd catch Nicholas doing it either!* He buried his head in his knees and groaned.

"Thomas, are you ill?"

Thomas jerked his head up to see Nicholas standing over him. Thomas was glad it was dark. He could feel his face glowing crimson.

"No, sir," he said.

"You're certain?" Nicholas said. "You've not been yourself lately, as far as I can see."

What could you possibly have seen except her? Thomas wanted to say. But he just shrugged.

"May I join you?" Nicholas asked.

Thomas nodded, and the doctor folded his lanky self onto the step beside him. There was a moment of silence, and Thomas remembered how easy it was to sit with Nicholas and not say anything. The memory made him sad, and he turned his head away.

"We haven't talked in some time," Nicholas said.

"You've been busy," Thomas said.

"We all have. Winifred most of all. She's already gone back to the hospital to be with the soldiers."

Thomas felt himself stiffen.

"I'm glad I found you here, though," Nicholas continued. "There's something I've been wanting to say to you—and heaven knows there's no chance with all those people." He gave a trembling half-smile toward the tavern door. "I appreciate the thought, but a party, for *me?* It hardly fits, does it?"

Thomas shook his head.

"You and I have been like partners since I came here," Nicholas said.

Thomas didn't answer, and this time the quiet didn't feel good. *Until* she *came,* he wanted to say. But he couldn't. Because that wasn't all. This was leading to good-bye, and that was someplace he didn't want to go.

"I'm not a man to make many friends," Nicholas went on, "but you're one of my few. Winifred's another. I hope while I'm gone that you two will be friends to each other. You're the strong ones. You'll need each other while everyone else depends on you."

Thomas could only stare at him. *Winifred and me, friends?* his thoughts were screaming.

"Winifred is not physically strong, though she won't admit it," Nicholas went on. "She has a . . . well, there's no need to go into that. I'm not as worried now, since your parents have been kind enough to offer her—"

"I don't want to talk about Winifred . . . if you don't mind, sir," Thomas said tightly.

Nicholas nodded. "I just want to be sure you understand why I'm going to the battlefront."

Thomas stared emptily at the silver buckles on his shoes.

"If it were up to me," Nicholas said, "I would stay right here. But I can't, you see."

"No," Thomas said in a rigid voice. "I don't see."

"I live my life by following God's will," Nicholas said. "It was God's will that I come to Williamsburg when all the other doctors left, and it is His will that I go to the soldiers and try to save lives."

"Everybody's talking about God's will now," Thomas said. He knew he sounded harsh, but he didn't care. "How do you know—?"

Nicholas put his hand on Thomas's arm. "I know because

I can almost feel God touching me with it, as if He were taking my arm."

"That wasn't what I was going to ask," Thomas said. His words were spurting out like sparks from a blacksmith's iron. "How do you know God even *cares* anymore?"

Nicholas looked startled, but he let Thomas go on.

"It doesn't seem like He cared about Alexander or Sam—they're gone. Or you—now you have to go. Or any of the soldiers. Or any of us!"

Nicholas let the fiery words soar through the air before he answered. "Have you talked to God about this, my friend?"

Thomas stopped. He was realizing something for the first time. "I guess I've stopped talking to Him," he said.

"Why?" Nicholas asked.

"I don't know!"

Suddenly, he couldn't sit on the steps next to Nicholas anymore. The anger was singeing his backbone as if it were Caroline's curling rod. He stood straight up and clenched his fists at his sides.

"I don't know!" he said again. "And I don't care!"

And before Nicholas could say anything, Thomas ran off into the inky darkness.

✢ ✦ ✢

Chapter Ten

homas wasn't sure where he was going until he ended up there—standing on the Chinese Bridge in the overgrown gardens of the Governor's Palace.

He sagged against the bridge railing and looked down into the canal. It was so dark and still that the water looked as if it had been lacquered on top, the way it had so many times when he and Caroline had come here to play.

How can it look the same, he thought, *when everything else is different?*

He turned and slid his back against the slats until he was sitting down on the bridge, leaning against the side and staring up into the black sky. He waited for the anger to run up and down his backbone again, but it didn't. Suddenly, all he felt was afraid.

I know I've changed a lot since the days when I first came here. At least I thought I had. People trust me now. They don't call me a bully and a brat anymore. But I feel like one inside again now. Thomas crossed his arms on his knees and rested his head on them. *What's the matter with me? I bet God's disappointed in me.*

Thomas propped his chin up on his arms and stared. Had he really told Nicholas he wondered if God even cared?

It sure doesn't seem like He does, Thomas thought. *Not like He used to.*

He closed his eyes. *God, I can't feel Your hand at all—not the way everybody else seems to. Can You just touch me— one time?*

Thomas got to his feet and stuck his hand up. He reached toward the ebony sky and stretched. He reached higher . . . and then he let his hand drop to his side. *This is stupid,* he thought, his cheeks tingling. *I hope nobody saw.*

Even as he thought it, there was a loud thud from the direction of the back of the Palace. Thomas tiptoed to the end of the bridge and squinted.

At first he didn't see anyone. But as he inched closer, the flickering of a candle in one of the windows turned the darkness under it a thin yellow. In that dim light, Thomas saw someone leaning over and struggling.

It was Winifred. She picked something up, only to drop it with a thump.

She's trying to pick up a piece of firewood, Thomas thought. *Why is that so hard?*

He edged away from the bridge and peered from behind a Chinese elm. Once again she picked up a piece of wood and tried to cradle it in her arms. But it was as if her limbs were wet noodles. The log tumbled to the ground, and Winifred gave a sigh Thomas could hear all the way across the garden.

"*She's not strong,*" Thomas could hear Nicholas saying. And then there was another noise. This time it was a kicking sound as Winifred drove her toe into the dropped log, followed by a cry of pain. Her noodle-arms dropped limply to her sides and she flung her head back to look at the sky.

Thomas froze behind the tree. He was pretty certain Winifred didn't want anyone to see her. And he wasn't going to do anything Winifred deWindt didn't want.

He pulled back in behind the tree to wait for her to leave. Suddenly, his eyes were pulled toward the window.

He caught the solid shape of someone very round walking by, and then stopping, and then leaning forward to look out, with the candle shining right in his face.

Thomas clapped his hands over his mouth. It was Xavier Wormeley.

Thomas his lip curl in disgust. *Too sick to even turn over, eh?* he thought. *And there he is strolling around the ward!* He stifled a snort. *I hope Winifred goes in and catches him!*

But there wasn't a chance of that. Xavier seemed to spot her standing with her back to him, and he skittered like a spooked squirrel away from the window.

And back to his pallet, Thomas thought with another lip curl. *What a fake!* The thought made him shake his head as he slipped out from the tree and made for home. *I've found someone who acts even stupider than I do.*

The rooster woke him with a rusty crow the next morning, Sunday, and as soon as Thomas's eyes opened, one nervous thought took its place in the center of his mind.

You were mean to Nicholas last night. Do you really want him to go away thinking you don't love God anymore?

"All right, all right!" he said out loud as he threw back his covers and set his feet down on the cool pine floor. "I'll go see him before I do chores."

He thought Nicholas had probably spent the night at the Governor's Palace with the soldiers after his party was over and would be leaving right after breakfast. Thomas hurried there as soon as he could pull on breeches and shoes.

The smell of almost-rancid bacon filled the ballroom ward as he stepped inside. *At least the ward smells better than it used to,* Thomas thought as he stood in the doorway and squinted into the gray light for Nicholas's familiar outline.

But the only person moving about was one with a long braid, moving from pallet to pallet like a busy bird. Thomas gnawed at the inside of his mouth and went toward her.

"Where is Nicholas?"

Winnie picked up a bowl of watery porridge from a tray. "Where do you think he is? On his way to Yorktown."

"No!" Thomas cried.

"Yes. And I'll thank you to keep your voice down. These men are sleeping."

"But he can't be gone! I have to talk to him!'

"Well, he is, and you can't, and that's the end of it!"

Thomas stared. She was always quick to answer, but this was different. Her voice cut through him like Louis's razor.

"Now, then," she said, "are you here to work or to argue with me?"

Thomas got his tongue working and turned on his heel as he answered. "Neither one," he said. And he hurried out of the Palace.

All through the service at the Bruton Parish Church that morning, Thomas felt the anger bristling up and down his backbone. He didn't hear any of the prayers or a word of gentle Reverend Pendleton's sermon, because his own thoughts shouted everything else down.

Nicholas left before I could apologize.

Now he probably hates me!

And all she *does is yell at me!*

He was chewing on those same thoughts as the sermon concluded and he felt his mother stand up beside him. Every eye in the church was on her as she smoothed her linen skirts with her little gloved hands and cleared her throat.

"As all of you know," she said, "a great battle is about to begin in Yorktown. I don't think there is a single one of us who doesn't know a boy or man who will be fighting in that battle."

A murmur went through the congregation.

"Many of us feel helpless in the face of such danger. But the ladies of Bruton Parish Church have discovered that we are not helpless. We can always go to God. And so we have organized a prayer vigil to be held here in the church from sunset tonight until dawn tomorrow. Each family may take an hour to stay awake here and pray for the safety of our young men. Would anyone like to be placed on our schedule?"

One man stood up. "In this prayer vigil of yours," he said, "you say we are to pray for the safety of our boys?"

"Yes," Mama said.

"I will not pray, Mistress Hutchinson," he said, "unless I may also pray for their victory at Yorktown!"

A few people began to clap.

"Certainly you may, sir," Virginia Hutchinson said. "May I put you down for an hour?"

"No," he said flatly. And then he smiled. "Put me down for two."

"Add the Wetherburns for two hours as well!" the tavern owner called out.

"Please put my name down, Mistress Hutchinson!"

"Ours, too!"

The church was alive with more noise than Thomas had ever heard in it. Thomas looked at his father, who was beaming. Then he twisted to look up into the servants' gallery where Malcolm and Patsy were grinning and nodding their heads.

But when his eyes landed on Caroline, Thomas's heart took a plunge. The Taylors were sitting very straight in their pew, close together and pale. A quick look around the church and Thomas knew why.

They were the only Loyalists left. So they were the only people not raising their hands and asking to be included in the vigil for the Patriots. Robert Taylor kept his chin level and his eyes up. But both his wife and Caroline were studying their palms.

And suddenly, so did Thomas.

As soon as the service was over, he wriggled through the throng of excited parishioners who crowded around Mama and Papa, and met Malcolm and Patsy outside the church. Robert and Betsy hurried out after him, with Caroline on their heels.

"May I stay a few minutes, please?" she said to her parents.

Her father's eyes passed over Thomas. "I would rather you didn't," he said stiffly.

Caroline winced, and Thomas felt a little stiff himself. *I'm glad I never told Papa what those men said to him that day at the mill,* he thought fiercely. *If he's going to make Caroline feel bad, then let him feel bad, too!*

Betsy Taylor took her husband's arm and whispered something in his ear. He nodded abruptly at Caroline and told her she could stay just a few minutes.

"Do I have some disease now?" Thomas whispered hoarsely to Caroline when they were gone.

"Yes," Malcolm said calmly. "It's called Patriotism. I told you, lad."

"Told me what?" Thomas said, his voice rising with the burning on his neck. "Why didn't he want you to stay here with us, Caroline?"

Caroline slipped her hand into Patsy's nervous one, and they all moved across the churchyard toward the Duke of Gloucester Street.

"It's the vigil," Caroline said. "Papa says the church was one place where we could all be at peace because the war wasn't being fought there." She looked sadly at the top of Patsy's head. "Now it is."

She dropped Patsy's hand and hoisted herself, Sunday skirts and all, up into a live oak that stood in the Courthouse yard. Thomas scrambled up after her, and Malcolm gave Patsy a boost before climbing up himself. Thomas settled on a limb with Caroline, but he didn't feel settled inside. No one did. Even Malcolm was chewing on a piece of grass with his narrow, black eyes closer together than ever as he watched Caroline.

"I want to pray, too!" she burst out suddenly. "My brother is out there fighting!"

"For the wrong side," Malcolm said.

Thomas looked away guiltily. He always got nervous when the conversation turned to Alexander.

"But he's still my brother!" she said.

"They don't care about that," Malcolm said. "All they want

to do is win the war. And I personally don't want to go to the church and pray about it. I want to go out and help them win!"

"You can't, Malcolm," Patsy said. "You're only 15."

"That's right," Thomas put in quickly.

"I know," Malcolm said, glowering at all of them. "You needn't keep remindin' me."

"And you don't have to keep reminding me that my father's a Loyalist and no one likes us anymore," Caroline said.

"I like you," Patsy said.

"A lot of good that does her," Malcolm said.

Caroline glared at him. "Malcolm, that was mean!"

"It's true, lassie!"

"I don't care what's true!" she said. "I'm sick of what's true."

They all stopped and went cold as stones. No one looked at anyone else as they examined their shoe tops and fingernails. Thomas chewed miserably at the inside of his mouth. His heart seemed to have sunk to a place where he couldn't even feel it beating anymore.

"I hate the war," Caroline said finally. "It makes *everybody* fight. Even us."

"Yeah," Patsy said faintly.

"There's going to be an even bigger fight when your father finds out you're working at the Patriot hospital," Malcolm said.

Caroline glared at him. "He won't find out unless someone tells him. He has too many other things to worry about to notice where I am."

"Well, I'll tell you one thing," Thomas said. "I'm not going to that stupid vigil."

Caroline turned to him, eyes open wide. "But, Thomas, it's your mama's vigil. You have to go."

"It would be a real slap in the face to your mother, lad," Malcolm said. He'd stopped chewing his grass and was looking hard at Thomas.

"I don't care," Thomas said stubbornly. "I'm never going to feel God's hand anyway, so what's the use?"

"God's hand?" Caroline said. "What do you mean?"

But Malcolm didn't give him a chance to answer. He tossed his grass over his shoulder and narrowed his eyes even more at Thomas. "And you never will, lad," he said, "if you believe things like that."

The anger tangled at the back of Thomas's neck, and he lurched forward on the branch, abruptly jostling both himself and Caroline. "When did you get ordained as a minister, *Malcolm?*" he said.

Malcolm went still. "I don't have to be a minister to know when something wrong has been said about God."

"It isn't wrong!"

"And I say it is!"

"Tom!" Caroline said. Her eyes went to Malcolm's face and back to his. "Tom, stop it now, please!"

"You tell *him* to stop it!" Thomas cried. "I'm not going to stop anything. I'm tired. I'm tired of—"

"Tired of what? Of bein' so stubborn you won't even listen to *God* anymore?" Malcolm said.

For a moment, Thomas forgot he was in a tree. He stood up on the branch and, hanging on to the one above, brought a fist up to his chest.

Slowly Malcolm got to his feet, too, and faced Thomas from the next branch as he held on. Thomas glared at him.

"Tom! Malcolm!" Caroline screamed. She clung to the limb. "Both of you stop!"

"If he takes it back, I'll stop!" Thomas cried.

"Take what back?" Malcolm said. His voice was even, but his free fist was ready. "Take what back?" he said again.

I don't know! Thomas wanted to cry. He didn't even know what he was so angry about. He only knew that if he didn't shout or punch or kick, he was going to explode. He clutched at the branch above him and clenched his other fist tighter.

"Tom, so help me," Caroline said, "if you start another fight with Malcolm, I will never, ever speak to you again."

Thomas felt himself breathing like a bull. Across from him, Malcolm's wiry form looked ready to spring.

"I mean it, Tom," she said.

I don't care if you never talk to me again! he wanted to scream at her. Except that it wasn't true. He did care about that—more than almost anything. He started to drop his fist to his side.

"You listen to her, lad," Malcolm said. "You won't listen to anybody else."

And then something did explode in Thomas. He lunged at Malcolm and felt first one and then the other silver-buckled shoe slide off the tree branch. He groped for something to hold on to, but there was only air—and he plummeted toward the ground.

✝ ✛ ✝

Chapter Eleven

The sky spun, and green and yellow trees blurred all around him. Then Thomas heard himself hit the ground.

The sky stopped spinning and the trees stopped whirling, and Thomas stared up and tried to breathe. But he couldn't.

He lay there as if he were frozen into a pile of snow. Black spots danced past his eyes. He closed his eyes and gasped.

Around him there were voices crying, "Thomas!" . . . "Tom!" . . . "Are you all right, lad?" He couldn't answer any of them. They seemed too far away to reach. He felt hands on him. Someone lifted his head. Someone grabbed his hand. Someone placed a hand on his stomach.

But none of it made sense as he groped for air. Not until another voice burst into the confusion and parted it as if she were parting tall grass.

"What's happened here, Scottie? Is someone hurt?"

Thomas felt everyone pull way, and he opened his eyes to see a pair of crisp blue-gray ones looking down at him.

Winifred deWindt's red braid slid over her shoulder and slapped him lightly on the cheek as she studied his face.

"The lad can't breathe!" Thomas heard Malcolm say.

"He's had the wind knocked out of him, is all," Winifred said. She took Thomas's face in her hands. "I want you to relax, sonny. All will be well. Don't fight it now. Just be calm. Deep breaths. That's it."

She was using her smooth pudding voice, the one she used with the patients. In spite of himself, Thomas watched her breathe in, and he breathed with her. His chest rattled and shook, but air filled his lungs.

"Not too fast, now," she said. "No gulping—that's it, sonny. Easy."

She watched as Thomas let the air go in and out. She nodded in her birdlike way as if that task were completed to her satisfaction, and then she began to run her hands down Thomas's arms.

"Does anything hurt?" she asked.

Thomas tried to shake his head, but it hurt. She nodded.

"You'll have a bit of a headache, I'll warrant you."

Thomas lay still as she finished examining his arms and started on his legs.

"Nothing hurts," he said.

"It will," she said matter-of-factly. "This time tomorrow you'll be hobbling worse than Francis Pickering with the bruises you're going to have. That will give you something to look forward to, eh?"

There was a sparkle in her eye, and as Thomas watched her probe at his head, he saw the same sparkle on her face. Not a smile. Just an acorn-shine.

"Do you feel like standing up now?" she said.

"Should he? Is he all right?"

Thomas remembered for the first time that Patsy, Caroline, and Malcolm were still there. Their faces came into focus above him, and he tried to grin. That hurt, too.

"Only hurts when you laugh, eh, sonny?" Winifred said. "Yes, I think he'll be all right to stand, with some help. Scottie, you take one arm, and you little missies take the other. That's it. Watch his back—"

As if they were pulling a baby calf to its feet for the first time, the rest of the Fearsome Foursome followed Winnie's directions and hauled Thomas up. The world reeled crazily for a moment, but it righted itself again.

"You have a scrape as red as a raspberry on your forehead, sonny," Winifred said. "You put some soapwort on that when you get home and then climb into bed. If it swells, I'll make a dovesdung plaster later. You should be fine by morning." She brushed off her skirts and then cocked her head at him like a sparrow. "But mind you, this is no excuse for not reporting for work tomorrow." With the shine still on her face, she turned and hurried toward the Palace Green as if the next patient she had to save was already calling out to her in her mind.

Thomas was still watching her when Caroline said, "Thank goodness you're all right, Tom." There were no dimples, no slice-of-melon smile. Her brown eyes were round and serious. "You could have really been hurt, you know."

Thomas looked down at his stocking toe, where the silver-buckled shoe had long since disappeared. "I know."

"I told you if you fought with Malcolm again, I couldn't speak to you anymore, Tom."

His head jerked up in time to see her gather up her

Sunday skirts and take off down the Duke of Gloucester, heels kicking at her petticoats as she ran. He could feel Malcolm looking at him, but he didn't look back. He didn't know what to say.

"I'm going to see Patsy to Mistress Lydia's," Malcolm said in a dead voice. "Can you get home on your own?"

"Yes," Thomas said tightly.

"Good, then. Don't forget what she said about the soapwort—"

"All *right!*" Thomas snapped.

When Malcolm was gone, Thomas headed miserably home.

As soon as he stepped into the house, Esther flew at him like a biddy with a brood of chicks. She produced not only soapwort and dovesdung, but enough blankets and chicken and dumpling soup and hot compresses for Thomas's forehead to stock the entire hospital ballroom ward for a week.

"What have you done to yourself?" she kept clucking to him as she bustled in and out and around Mama, who sat on his bed and stroked his hands.

"Do I need to send Malcolm for your papa?" she said. "He's at a meeting at Wetherburn's Tavern."

For the first time, Thomas saw that Malcolm was lurking in the doorway, watching him like a wary fox.

"No!" Thomas said. "I'll be fine. Mistress Winifred said that I just need rest."

That seemed to carry as much weight as an order from General Washington. They gave him one more set of pats and kisses and hot compresses and hustled out of the room— *whispering as if I were about to die of the small pox,* Thomas thought as the door clicked shut behind them. The door opened once again and Malcolm brought in another log for the fire that had already turned the room into an oven.

"I'm warm enough," Thomas said to him.

He expected Malcolm to grunt and stomp out, but instead he came over to the bed and said, "Are you sure you'll be all right, lad? I can stay with you."

A lump formed in Thomas's throat. He wanted to say yes. He wanted to patch things up with Malcolm and go back to the way things used to be. He opened his mouth . . . and then Malcolm opened his.

"All right, then, lad, have it your own stubborn way. I guess when you're ready to listen to somebody, you'll let us all know."

And *then* he grunted and stomped out of the room.

Thomas slept fitfully all afternoon. He awoke at dusk, and he could see the outline of Papa standing beside his bed.

"We're going to be all night at the vigil, Thomas," his father said softly. "Esther and Malcolm are going with us, but Otis will be out in the kitchen. Just ring the bell for him if you need anything. But ring it loud—you know he isn't hearing as well as he did."

"Yes, sir," Thomas said.

"There's a candle here by your bed, too, if you need it."

Thomas nodded and waited for his father to leave, but Papa stood there, looking right into him.

"Shall I say any prayers on your behalf at the vigil?"

Prayers, Thomas thought guiltily. *I haven't done much praying lately.* But two thoughts did come to his mind. Sam and the Taylors. Maybe it was time to tell Papa about that.

"Pray for Sam to come home," Thomas said first.

Papa sighed. "Thomas, we have talked about this."

"He's still alive—"

"We shouldn't waste our prayers, Thomas," Papa said sharply. "Is there anything else?"

"No!" Thomas said just as sharply. And he turned his head away. He heard the door close softly.

Prayers, Thomas thought bitterly as he listened to the fading footsteps. *God? Are You there? Because if You are, I can't hear You anymore. And I certainly can't feel You touching me.*

All he could feel was the tear that trickled down his cheek.

It was completely dark the next time he woke up. The room was still with the chill of an early fall evening, and Thomas wondered what had awakened him. A moment later, he had his answer as someone pounded impatiently on the front door.

Why doesn't Otis answer it? he thought.

Thomas sat up and reached for the bell and then grunted to himself. If Otis couldn't hear the pounding, he certainly wasn't going to hear the bell either.

I'm tired of being in bed anyway, he thought as he threw back the pile of blankets. The floor seemed to shift under his feet, but he made his way slowly out of his room and down the steps. The pounding was still going on when he reached the front door and pulled it open.

Lit by the firebrand he carried, a Virginia militiaman in buff breeches and dark-blue coat looked down at him. The glow of the flame revealed a sausage curl on either side of his tricornered hat and a face that was all business.

"Good evening," the officer said in a chilly voice. He looked past Thomas over his shoulder. "Is there anyone home?"

"I'm home," Thomas answered.

The officer looked down at him curiously, and Thomas followed his eyes. He was wearing only his nightshift and a bandage on his head. Thomas folded his arms across his chest and tried to will his face not to turn red.

The officer gave him one more cursory look and then reached into his satchel and pulled out a roll of parchment.

Thomas went cold as he watched the officer unroll the paper and study it. Was it about Sam? Was this news? Bad news?

"Is there a Malcolm Donaldson living here?" the officer asked.

For a moment, Thomas couldn't answer. His head was spinning. *Malcolm? Then this isn't about Sam!*

"I suppose I should come back when the master of the house is here," the officer said impatiently. He rerolled the paper and opened his satchel.

"No!" Thomas said quickly. "I can help you!"

The man gave him another doubtful look. "I have papers here for one Malcolm Donaldson. It has come to our attention that he is 15, which means he must soon serve his time in the militia." The officer drew himself up. "As you know, Virginia needs him now more than ever."

The officer glared down his thin nose at him as Thomas's mind raced. *He's come to take Malcolm! He's going to make him go away—like everyone else!*

"What are those papers?" Thomas said, barely recognizing his own voice.

"These explain what will happen on his 16th birthday," the man said brusquely. "Where is this Malcolm Donaldson?"

Thomas's mind took one more spin, and then he looked the man square in the eye. "I am Malcolm Donaldson," he said.

The officer didn't blink. He simply snapped the rolled parchment forward and waited. Thomas reached out and took it—and he hoped the officer couldn't see his hand trembling.

"Read it and be ready," the officer said. "It will take every able-bodied man to win this battle at Yorktown."

"Yes, sir," Thomas murmured.

The officer took one more look at Thomas's nightshift and said, "See you get all the rest you can, young man. You shall need it."

When he was gone, Thomas leaned against the closed door and shook. The paper in his hand burned his palm like a lie burning his tongue.

I did lie, he thought. *I lied to a military officer!*

Feeling as if he were going to be sick, Thomas hurried through the hall and up the stairs. His heart was racing as he snatched up the candle in its holder and dashed toward the fireplace. There was still enough of a flame for him to light the candle to read by.

On the day of his 16th birthday, one Malcolm Donaldson will be called upon by a soldier of the Virginia Militia and presented with orders for his call to duty. He must be prepared with a knapsack with provisions for service in battle: one blanket, one set of rations . . .

The paper blurred in front of Thomas's eyes, and he

turned it over with a fierce slap. *Provisions for service in battle,* he thought. *They want to take Malcolm to battle. Just like Sam. Just like Alexander. Just like Nicholas.*

Thomas closed his eyes against the sting and tried to imagine the officers coming to take Malcolm away. *"Do you have your knapsack, soldier?"* they would say. *"Are you prepared for battle?"*

And Malcolm will be ready, Thomas thought. *Because he wants to go. He's said it a hundred times.*

Thomas closed his eyes again, but this time he saw only himself as Malcolm marched off with the soldiers. Thomas crumpled the paper in his thick hands. "Please, God!" he cried out. "Please don't let them take Malcolm, too!"

He put his head down to cry, but no tears came. Instead, there was only a thought. *God can't stop this. The soldiers are coming for Malcolm, and God will let them take him, just like He did everyone else. No one can stop it.* Thomas felt the crumpled points of the parchment digging into his hands, and he stared at it. *No one except me,* the thought said.

He looked from the candle to the paper and back again only once before he smoothed the parchment over his lap. He could hear himself breathing as he touched it to the candle flame. And then all he heard was the gentle crackling as Malcolm's instructions turned to ashes.

✞ ⋅✞⋅ ✞

Chapter Twelve

The house was alive at dawn the next day with the noise of voices and something being dragged up the stairs.

Thomas hauled his aching muscles out of bed to peek out the door. *Mistress Winifred was right,* he thought as he cringed against the pain in his shoulder. *I do feel like Francis Pickering!* But that thought disappeared the moment he looked through the crack in the door, and then flung it open.

"Right up here now, Malcolm," Esther was saying as she backed past Thomas's room toward a doorway down the hall. "And careful you don't damage it."

Thomas saw that she was talking about a battered trunk Malcolm was dragging toward the open doorway.

"What's that?" Thomas asked.

"Major deWindbag's belongin's," Malcolm said curtly. "She sent to Pennsylvania for them. Looks like she's stayin' a while."

"Stayin' where?"

"Here," Malcolm said and continued down the hall with

the beat-up old trunk and steered it into the room.

"Here?" Thomas said. "Why?"

"Because your mama and papa asked her to," Esther clucked from the doorway. "She ought to be in here a-sleepin' right now, bein' up all night like she was, a-prayin' and then a-doctorin'. But no, she's already at the hospital—which is where you need to get to, Malcolm, soon as you're done here and have your chores finished."

"I know, Esther," Thomas heard him say. Thomas poked his head out to listen further—just in time to be met by Esther's hawkish eyes.

"What are you doing up, Thomas Hutchinson?" she said, stalking toward him like an angry mother goose. "You get back into that bed at once."

"Mistress Winifred told me I'd be well enough to work this morning!" Thomas cried.

Esther stopped in her tracks and pursed her lips. "All right, then," she said. "If Mistress Winifred says so, then I suppose it must be all right." She bustled away.

Malcolm slipped out of the room as Esther disappeared into it, and he started past Thomas's door.

"She's staying *here?*" Thomas said to him.

"So?" Malcolm said. "What's the matter with that?"

Thomas felt his mouth drop open further. "I thought you didn't like her any more than I do," he said.

Malcolm shrugged and took the stairs down two at a time. Thomas was sure he'd never felt emptier inside.

Even though she had invaded his home now, at least he had Winifred to thank for one thing, Thomas decided in the next few days. She kept him busy so he didn't have to be alone with the thoughts that kept blowing back into his head like ashes whenever he wasn't busy with something else.

He worked hard—feeding patients, delivering medicines, scrubbing floors, and assisting Winifred. But even slaving from dawn till dusk didn't chase away his nagging thoughts. His troubles slapped him in the face with every person he saw.

Caroline made sure she was off running messages most of the time. When she was there, she busied herself reading to the soldiers. Her voice was chilly when she talked to Thomas. Patsy, of course, copied Caroline.

Malcolm kept his distance, too. The only thing he said to Thomas was, "I can turn the patients by myself. You have other things to do."

And his father . . . Thomas avoided him whenever he could. At dinner he kept his eyes on his porringer. If Papa couldn't believe that Sam was alive, there was no reason to talk to him.

Old Francis was the only one who didn't seem to be mad at him. But he was too busy to do much of anything but mix medicines and cough. When Thomas suggested he take some of his own licorice troches, the apothecary nearly snapped his head off.

And then there was Winifred. She seemed to have forgotten how gentle and kind she had been to Thomas the day he was hurt. She barked at Thomas louder and more often than ever.

She just thinks she can get away with it now that Nicholas isn't here, making eyes at her, Thomas thought.

And that wasn't the worst of it. Not only did he have to see her all day at the hospital, but he had to sit across from her at supper every night as well—and sometimes pass her in the halls of the Hutchinson house or look up from his book in their parlor to see her staring into their fireplace.

There's no getting away from her, he told himself one day as he was filling up the medicine cabinet yet again with Francis's powders and syrups. *She's as bad as Xavier Wormeley, hanging about.*

Xavier himself still refused to get off his pallet. He lay there all day, moaning loudly and complaining every time Louis got something he didn't. The only time they had any peace was when the fat man was sleeping. And even then his snores flapped his jowls and vibrated through the ward.

Thomas was sitting with Louis one afternoon, wiping the sweat of still another fever off the Frenchman's brow, when Xavier let out a sleeping snort that made them both jump. Louis's face eased into a grin.

"He's a noisy one, isn't he?" Thomas said.

Louis nodded, and Thomas cocked his head.

"You understand English, don't you?" Thomas said.

Louis nodded, his feverish eyes glowing.

"But you can't speak it? You can only speak French?"

Louis held up his thumb and forefinger, almost pinched together.

"Just a little bit," Thomas said. "You can speak English just a little bit."

Louis nodded happily.

Thomas wrung out his cloth in the basin. "Would you like this on your head again?" Thomas asked.

Louis shook his head and then pressed his palms together and opened them out.

"You want me to read to you?" Thomas said.

"Oui, si vous plait," Louis said.

"I'll find a book," Thomas said. "The ladies have brought in stacks of them."

He started to get up, but Louis pointed to the bag on the chair. Thomas looked at it nervously. "You don't want me to shave you, do you?"

Louis shook his head, and Thomas dug into the bag. His fingers curled around a small book, and he pulled it out.

"I can't read French, Louis," Thomas said.

But Louis shook his head and pointed, and Thomas studied the book's front cover. *The Holy Bible.*

"Oh," Thomas said. "I've read this book. Well, some of it. I was reading it with my teacher, Alexander Taylor, before he . . ."

His voice faded. Why did everything hurt?

"Monsieur Thomas?"

Thomas looked up to find Louis watching him with sad eyes. He ran his finger from his eye down his cheek.

"Am I sad?" Thomas said. "No, no, I want to read. What would you like to hear?"

Louis reached for the Bible and, closing his eyes, he opened the book and dropped his finger on the page. He held it there as he opened his eyes and looked at Thomas.

"Just start right there?" Thomas said.

Louis nodded, and then with a slow peaceful breath, he settled into the pallet and waited. Thomas looked down the page at the tiny printing to the verse Louis had picked out. He'd never read the Bible out loud. He didn't always understand what it meant when he heard it read in church. He'd always had Alexander to explain it to him.

But Louis looked expectant and happy as he waited for Thomas to start, so Thomas chewed his lip a moment and then began to read.

"'Now Naaman, captain of the host of the King of Syria,

was a great man,'" Thomas read. "'He was also a mighty man in valour, but he was a leper.'"

Thomas read on, about how Naaman heard that a holy man named Elisha in Israel had a cure for leprosy. Naaman, he read to Louis, went to Israel to Elisha's house. But instead of coming to Naaman himself, the holy man sent instructions for Naaman to dip himself in the Jordan River seven times. Disappointed that Elisha didn't come to him and give him the cure in person, Naaman grew angry.

Thomas looked at Louis. "He was mad just because the cure wasn't the way he expected?"

Louis nodded as if he hated to admit it.

Naaman, it seemed to Thomas as he continued to read, felt that he could have just as easily washed himself in the rivers at home, rather than coming all this way for nothing.

Thomas looked impatiently at Louis. "So how did it turn out? Did he die of leprosy?"

"No," Louis said. He pointed his hands as if he were diving.

"He dipped in the Jordan anyway," Thomas said.

Louis bobbed his head, and then he held out his arms and smiled at them.

"And then he was healed," Thomas said.

"Oui," said Louis. He waved at the Bible, and Thomas read on.

"'Naaman said I now know that there is no other God in all the earth.'"

When Thomas looked up at Louis again, the Frenchman was closing his eyes and smiling peacefully. His forehead was dry and he gave a long, easy breath.

"That fever has broken," said a husky voice behind him.

Thomas looked up to see Winifred standing there. He jumped up, scattering the water basin in one direction and the Bible in the other.

"He just wanted me to read to him," Thomas stammered.

Before Winnie could answer, there was a roar from the next pallet.

"What's all this racket?" Xavier cried, drool hanging from his lower lip. "Can't a sick man have some peace and quiet?"

"A sick man can, Mr. Wormeley," Winifred said as she bent over and picked up the basin and handed it back to Thomas. "But you can't."

"I refuse to put up with these insults another moment!" Xavier cried. "I am very ill! When will I get care?"

"You're getting all the care I can spare," Winifred said crisply. "I offered to have a young lady read to you this morning, and you sent her packing."

Xavier's jowls stopped jiggling for a minute. "Do you mean that Taylor girl?"

"Yes," Winifred said absently. She was busy straightening Louis's blankets, but Xavier suddenly had Thomas's full attention.

"The girl's a Loyalist!" Xavier cried.

"I don't care if she's a cow with two heads, Mr. Wormeley," Winifred said without looking at him. "She works hard. That's all that counts."

"Don't let her come near me again. She'd be run out of town if I had my way—and her stinking family with her!"

The basin clattered from Thomas's hand again, and he stiffened, ready to lunge at the fat militiaman. But a set of fingers curled around his arm and held him in place—not by their strength but by the gentle warning squeeze they gave him. Thomas looked up at Winifred in surprise, but she had turned to stare down at Xavier.

"If you can't live with her being here, Wormeley," she said, "then suppose you go, eh?"

She didn't shout, the way Thomas wanted to. And she didn't hurl herself at him the way Thomas was itching to. But Thomas could feel the anger pulsing through her as she held on to his arm. He didn't pull away.

For a long moment Xavier stared back at her out of his poke-hole eyes. His overripe face had grown purple, and Thomas wondered if he were even breathing. But when Winifred didn't move, Xavier flopped over like a blowfish and lay with his back to them all.

Slowly, Winifred let go of Thomas's arm. Before he could move away, they heard a chuckle from the pallet below them. Both of them looked down to see Louis lying on his side with his thin cheeks blown out with air and his eyes squinting like a pig's. Winifred put her hand over her mouth, her eyes merrily shooting sparks over her fingers.

"He's imitating Mr. Wormeley!" Thomas whispered to her.

Winifred bobbed her head. "And a fine job he's doing of it, too, sonny!" she whispered back.

It was a happy moment—the first one Thomas had felt in a long time. Even as Winifred bustled back to work and Francis wheezed for Thomas to make yet another trip to the apothecary shop, he kept the image of Louis with his puffed up cheeks and Winifred with her almost-smile in his mind, and he felt a glimmer of happiness. And it would last until supper that night, when Mama made her announcement.

✝ ◆ ✝

Chapter Thirteen

It was the first night with a real chill in the air, and Malcolm came into the dining room several times to add wood to the fire. Thomas tried to concentrate on his potato soup so he wouldn't have to look at him. It was like a bee sting every time Malcolm wouldn't meet his eyes. He missed the messages he and Malcolm used to send to each other without saying a word.

But Mama was watching the servant boy, and the last time he left, she said, "Thomas, lock the door."

"What?"

"Lock the door! Hurry, before he comes back!"

"But Mama—"

"Thomas, humor your mother," Papa said. His blue eyes were twinkling as he spooned more soup into his mouth and watched his wife with amusement.

Mystified, Thomas turned the latch on the door and scurried back to his seat. Winnie was holding her spoon in midair and looking at Virginia Hutchinson as if perhaps a medical examination might be in order.

Mama leaned forward with her gray eyes shining. "All right, then. We're going to have a party!"

Thomas looked at her blankly. *Why is that so big? We have parties all the time.*

"A party, ma'am?" Winnie said. "With a battle about to begin and all of us so busy?"

"That is precisely the time to have a party!" Mama said. "And we have a *very* good reason."

Papa chuckled. "Tell them what it is, my dear."

Mama folded her dainty hands under her chin. "John was looking over Malcolm's indenture papers and discovered that October 13th is Malcolm's birthday. His 16th birthday."

Thomas had to grip his spoon to keep it from clattering into his bowl. His thoughts nearly strangled him: *We can't let the whole world know it's Malcolm's 16th birthday. The militia will come after him for sure!*

"Thomas?" Mama said. She was looking at him curiously. "I thought you would be pleased about this."

Thomas glued his eyes to a chunk of potato floating in his bowl. "I think Mistress deWindt is right. It doesn't seem right—not with the war so close."

There was a disappointed silence. Thomas looked up at Winnie, to find her gazing at him with both auburn eyebrows pointed up like arrowheads.

"Hmmm," she said softly, and went back to her soup.

"Malcolm has become almost like another son to us," Papa said brusquely. "I think we owe him this attention."

Thomas could feel The Look boring into him. He nodded stiffly.

"Now, then," Mama said, "we have preparations to make.

Since I'm working at the hospital so much, Esther will be in charge of most of them. She'll be asking you to do a few things, Thomas. But please remember, it's a secret."

I'll have no trouble with that part, he thought miserably. He put the potato in his mouth and felt it turn to sawdust.

In the days that followed, Thomas wished that time would stop altogether and Malcolm's birthday would never come and people would forget it even existed.

But there wasn't a chance of that happening. Suddenly, it seemed all he heard about was the surprise party.

One morning Esther had Thomas running to the bake shop at Raleigh Tavern to order tarts and cakes before he even went to the hospital. Another evening when he came home ready to drop in his tracks, she made him run to Wetherburn's with a list of music their musicians were to play for Malcolm's celebration. She even made him stand in for Malcolm at the tailor's for a fitting of the new suit they were having made for him.

The only good thing about it, Thomas decided, was Caroline. She was so excited about delivering the invitations and helping his mother plan the decorations, she seemed to have forgotten that she was barely speaking to Thomas. One day she was chattering to him about it while they helped Louis with his dinner.

"What is this incessant yakking about a birthday party?" Xavier cried from his pallet. "There is a war going on! Who is celebrating a birthday in the middle of a war?"

Caroline turned to him and said politely, "Malcolm Donaldson. On the 13th."

Thomas poked her with his elbow.

"What?" she said.

He shook his head and nodded toward Xavier.

The fat man observed them thoughtfully out of his poke-hole eyes for a moment and then growled, "There will be no more talk of parties, do you hear?"

But that didn't slow down Caroline. Four days before the party, they were sitting on the Chinese Bridge at dinner time, swinging their legs over the canal when she brought it up for the thousandth time.

"You don't seem excited about this party one bit," she said. "Are you and Malcolm still fighting? Is that what it is?"

"No," Thomas said glumly. "He doesn't talk to me at all."

She let her hands fall into her lap, and her brown eyes looked sad.

"We used to have so much fun, Tom. Right here on this bridge."

Thomas nodded. "We had good games. Playing Vikings and princesses—"

"—and soldiers. You were always the best at them, Tom. I mean, I thought them up, but you could act them out so well, I thought it was real." Her eyes lit up. "Do it now!"

"What?"

"Do it now. You be the officer and I'll be . . . I'll be some lowly soldier."

"Just . . . you mean right here?"

"What better place? Come on!"

She gathered up her skirts and sprang to her feet, and Thomas couldn't help jumping up with her.

"Sir," she said in a deep voice. She drew herself up at attention and gave him a salute. "I am reporting for duty."

"And it's about time, soldier!" Thomas said gruffly. He

clicked his heels together and surveyed the Palace Gardens with a serious, searching gaze. "The enemy is already approaching from—"

Thomas stopped and felt his eyes spring open. Striding out the back door of the Palace was a slender figure with faded blond hair. Thomas grabbed Caroline's hand and yanked her down.

"I don't remember this in the game!" she said.

"Shhh! It's your father!"

Caroline peered through the slats of the bridge railing.

"What's he doing here?" Caroline whispered.

"What if he finds you?"

She didn't answer, but Thomas saw her fingers tighten around the slats.

"He wouldn't really punish you, would he?" Thomas whispered nervously. "I mean, not too bad."

"Shhh!" she said. "He's coming this way!"

It did indeed look as if Robert Taylor was headed right for the Chinese Bridge.

He could hear Caroline swallow. "He told me if I had anything to do with any Patriots besides you and Malcolm and Patsy, he would lock me in my room."

"He wouldn't!" *And to think I was going to ask Papa to do something about the people who insulted him*, he added in his mind.

And then they heard a shout—one that came from heaven, as far as Thomas was concerned.

"Mr. Taylor, good morning! Can I help you, sir?"

Robert Taylor turned to face Malcolm, who was running toward him from the back of the Palace, face fixed firmly into a big, square smile. Caroline squeezed Thomas's arm until he thought it would pop off as they watched the two of them talk.

"What do you think they're saying?" Thomas hissed.

"Shhh!" Caroline hissed back.

"Whatever it is, I think Malcolm just saved you."

Robert Taylor nodded politely to Malcolm and strode off away from the Palace toward the Green. Only when he had disappeared did Caroline turn and plump down against the railing, with Thomas beside her.

"I love Malcolm," she said, huffing out air. "I will love him forever!"

But Thomas looked down at his hands.

"What is it, Tom?" Caroline asked.

"It's no good anymore. You even have to hide from your father."

"He's gone now," she said. "And I'm not going to let anything spoil what is good. We're going to go to Malcolm's party and—"

Thomas scrunched up his mouth.

"To-om!" Caroline said. "We finally have a chance to do something fun, and you spend the whole time pouting. Then it's no fun at all."

Thomas looked at her sideways. "Why?"

"Because," she said. She sighed and toyed with her fingers. "Because it's not fun unless we're doing it together."

Suddenly, he wanted to tell her what Malcolm's 16th birthday really meant. He was no closer to devising a plan for what to do, and Caroline always had such good ideas.

But instead he blurted out, "I don't want Malcolm to turn 16!"

She stared at him for a moment, and then her eyes seemed to understand. "Sometimes I look at him and he seems more like Alexander and Sam than like us." She lowered her voice. "I think he even shaves his face now, Tom."

Thomas wriggled his shoulders uncomfortably. He wanted to tell her so much.

"Even Patsy isn't sad about Malcolm growing up," she said, "and who should want him to stay the same more than her?"

An idea—a mean little idea—flickered in the corner of Thomas's mind. Patsy was Caroline's best girlfriend and a good reason for Caroline to try and stop the party.

Thomas sniffed. "The sooner he gets to be a man, the sooner he goes on with his own life and doesn't have time for her."

"No!" Caroline cried—just as Thomas had known she would. "That won't happen! Malcolm will always be here to take care of her!"

"Then tell them to call off this party!" Thomas said.

"What good will that do, Tom?"

Thomas didn't have the slightest idea. It had seemed to be such a good plan when he'd started, but now he felt small and mean and miserable.

"Never mind," he said lamely. "Just forget I said anything."

"Why *did* you say those terrible things?"

"Because I'm stupid," Thomas said.

"You're not stupid, Tom. That's why I don't understand."

He was waiting for her to plant her hands onto her hips the way she always did, but he was surprised when she folded her arms miserably across her chest. She looked as if she were trying hard not to let her face pucker.

Once more Thomas wanted to tell her. Caroline was the

one person who seemed to understand him the best. He could trust her.

But he waited too long.

"Are you just doing this to be spiteful because you and Malcolm are mad at each other?" Caroline said. The hands were on the hips now and fire was in the eyes. "You're not a hateful person, Tom Hutchinson. I hate to see you acting like one."

And then she scrambled up and ran away.

"Caroline, wait!" he called after her. "I'm sorry!"

He ran from the bridge and charged toward the Palace.

"You're both going to be worse than sorry, lad."

Thomas stopped and felt Malcolm coming up behind him.

"Her father was here lookin' for her just now."

Thomas turned to face him. "And you told him she wasn't here, didn't you?"

"Yes, I did, lad. But I won't do it again. I don't like lyin'. That was never somethin' we did, the Fearsome Foursome."

"But you had to lie or Caroline would have been in trouble."

"Then she shouldn't be here, should she?" Malcolm said. He shook his shaggy head and turned away. "I have more important things to worry about."

"You won't tell on her!" Thomas shouted after him.

But Malcolm didn't answer.

Thomas didn't see Caroline all afternoon, and he could think of nothing else all through supper and Evening Prayer. He excused himself early for bed just to get away from all the eyes.

It was hard to fall asleep. It seemed he had only just

drifted off when a noise awakened him. He sat straight up in bed with his mind reeling.

Have they come for Malcolm? He still has three days left!

But it wasn't a pounding on the door. It was a pounding in the sky. And at first he thought it was thunder.

But there was no smell of threatening rain. And no wind or lightning. He saw that when he ran to the window. Still there it was again—a pounding in the sky.

Grabbing a blanket to wrap around his nightshift, Thomas slipped out of his room and down the stairs to the back porch. If anyone else had been awakened by the noise, they weren't getting up for it . . . except the thin, shadowy figure that stood atop the fence rail with his hand shielding his eyes.

Swallowing his pride, Thomas hurried toward Malcolm and joined him on the fence.

"What is it?" he asked.

Malcolm pointed, and Thomas watched. In another moment, the sky seemed to explode with fire and then was dark and still again.

"Cannons," Malcolm said softly. "The battle at Yorktown has begun."

✠ ✦ ✠

Chapter Fourteen

"You mean, that's the war?" Thomas said.

"Right before our eyes."

The sky lit up again, and Thomas was sure he felt the vibration in his feet.

He was seeing the war. And hearing it. And feeling it. It had always seemed so far away before.

But now they were shooting cannons—at people like Alexander and Sam.

"I wish I were there," Malcolm said. His eyes were still aimed fiercely at the sky and his voice matched his gaze. "I haven't fired a single shot to help."

Malcolm's voice suddenly broke off, and he jerked from the fence and stalked toward the kitchen. Startled red and orange leaves scattered around his feet and then settled to the ground again.

But Thomas's mind couldn't settle, even after Malcolm slammed the kitchen door behind him.

He wants *to go,* he thought miserably. *If he ever finds out I didn't give him that information, he'll hate me.*

But I would hate it more if he went away—and was—

"He won't go away," Thomas blurted out into the night.

He didn't know what to do next. He thought for a moment of praying, but he pushed the idea aside. What was the use? Things only seemed to get worse and worse anyway. God's hands were nowhere to be seen.

The cannons boomed on until Thomas couldn't watch them anymore. He turned his back to the battle sky, but he could still see the fire light up first the front of the stable, then the side of the laundry, then the eaves of the house. Following the light up to the roof of the Hutchinsons' house, Thomas's eyes sprang open. He was sure he saw someone sitting up there.

He wasn't sure why, but Thomas pulled his blanket around him and hurried into the house and up the two flights of stairs to the attic. The tiny attic window was already open, and Thomas had to squeeze to get out of it and onto the roof. But he nearly turned around and wriggled back through when he saw Winifred deWindt.

His first step out onto the shingles had been clumsy, and she turned and saw him before he had a chance to get away.

"Hello, sonny," she said. "Come to watch the show?"

"Yes, ma'am," he said.

"There seems to be an empty seat," she said.

Thomas shrugged and made his way across the roof and sat down beside her. "So the war has begun," she said "I suppose we have to let God have His free hand now."

"I don't think God has anything to do with that," Thomas said, pointing to the cannon fire.

"What makes you say that?" Winifred said.

"God didn't send my brother or Caroline's brother or

Nicholas out there to get . . . shot at." Thomas shrugged again. "Not unless He doesn't care."

"Hmmm," she said.

Suddenly, Thomas was irritated. He could feel it climbing up the back of his neck, and it felt better than the fear. "Why do you always say 'Hmmm'?"

Winifred pulled her cape tighter around her and flipped her braid. "I suppose I say it when I've had a thought that I know someone else doesn't want to hear." She looked at him, her eyes crisp. "I'll bet you thought I say everything I think, didn't you?"

Thomas couldn't lie to those eyes. He nodded. And to his amazement, she chuckled. It was a throaty, husky sound, like a horse nickering.

"When I see somebody saying one thing when I know they feel another, I often keep my mouth shut," she said. "Especially when I know they'll figure it out sooner or later."

"Why don't you just tell them?" Thomas asked.

"Because sometimes people aren't ready to hear it. I know I'm like that—just pretend to be thinking one thing so I won't have to think another. And I don't want anyone telling me otherwise or I'll snap their head off. Now you believe that part, don't you, sonny?"

Thomas snorted. "Yes!"

She chuckled again. "I think I've said enough prayers for tonight. God probably has plenty of other people to listen to. There isn't one of us who doesn't have someone we love out there in the middle of all that."

She got up suddenly and nodded good night to him and disappeared through the window.

The next morning Esther made Thomas stay behind after Malcolm left for the hospital.

"I have to tell you about our plan," she said, glancing out the window like a spy to be sure he was well out of earshot.

"What plan?" Thomas said.

"To surprise Malcolm for his party." She rubbed her hands together and lowered her voice. "Now, that evening when he leaves the hospital, you and Mistress Caroline are going to tell Malcolm that he has to go to the leathersmith's for Master John. You walk him along until Master John himself comes by in the buggy and takes Malcolm away—" Esther clapped gleefully "—to the tailor's shop! Then you can run back here and get dressed yourself and meet us all at Wetherburn's. Now do you have that, Thomas?"

Thomas was certain she could see his heart slamming against the inside of his chest as he nodded and escaped from the kitchen.

What am I going to do? he thought all the way to the hospital. *I can't let this happen.*

His mind was still spinning when he walked into the hospital ballroom and Winifred barked, "You're late, sonny."

But Thomas just stood and stared. The ward was alive with activity. Malcolm pushed patient-laden pallets closer together, ladies stacked new supplies of bandages and blankets in piles in the corners, and Francis crammed even more jars and bottles into the medicine cabinet. Caroline flitted past him with two big baskets of bread, and Patsy followed, dragging a sack of flour.

"It isn't going to get done with you standing there, sonny!" Winifred said as she sailed by. "You saw that battle last night, and after a battle comes casualties."

"The wounded are coming here?" Thomas asked.

Winifred stopped to look at him. "What did you think we had this hospital for? The likes of Xavier Wormeley?"

Of course not, Thomas thought. He'd known all along that there would be soldiers coming here from the battle. But now it was real.

He felt even more frightened than he had last night with the cannons lighting up the sky. He wanted to run—and take Malcolm and Caroline and Patsy with him—back to the Palace Gardens where they had only pretended at war.

"Come with me, and we'll bring in more pallets," Winifred said briskly. "Later today I'll show you how to change a dressing."

"On a bullet wound?"

"Not on a stubbed toe," she said dryly. She bustled on, rubbing her arms as she hurried down the rows of pallets with Thomas tripping over himself to keep up.

She pushed a pallet toward him with her foot and spread it on the floor.

"Louis, what do you think you're doing?" he heard her say.

Thomas looked up. Louis was standing in front of Winifred with his arms outstretched as if he were waiting for her to drop a pallet into it.

"*Si vous plait, Mademoiselle* Ween-ee-fred," he said, and then gave her a charming smile.

"What are you talking about?" she said briskly. "You have a pallet. Now lie down on it before you fall down!"

Louis shook his head and held his arms out insistently.

"I think he wants to help," Thomas said.

"You're still sick, Louis!"

"He doesn't look sick to me," Thomas said.

Winifred looked at Louis impatiently, and then her face smoothed. "He doesn't, does he?" She crossed her arms. "All right, but if you feel the least bit woosey, you tell sonny."

Thomas nodded. The minute her back was turned, he looked at Louis and grinned. Louis stuck out his thumb and turned it upward.

"We'll work together," Thomas said to him. "I'll carry them in and you'll unroll them."

"Wake up, Jowls! There's no time for sleeping now. We need you out of the way!"

Winifred stalked over to the pallet where Xavier Wormeley lay snoring.

"I need my sleep!" Xavier growled at her.

"You need to get up off your fat rumpus. In fact—" she yanked the blanket off of him "—you can not only get up, but you can help. Look at Louis. Just yesterday recovered from his last fever and he's unrolling pallets. Get up, now. The activity will do you good." She gave his rotund form a disapproving look and turned to unroll another pallet.

"I have had *enough* of your insolence, woman!" Xavier roared.

"And I've had enough of your fakery," she said. She didn't turn to face him. She didn't raise her voice. But Thomas saw the anger harden her face.

"Faking am I?" Xavier said. "You can't see suffering when it's right in front of you. I'll show you who is ill and needs attention!"

With a gasping bellow, Xavier gathered his purple sleeping jacket around him and struggled to a sitting position. His face turned scarlet as he gave himself a heave and stood up—only to tumble straight to the floor with a thud that shook the Palace.

"Oh, my!" Thomas's mother said as she rushed over from the bandage pile. "What's happened?"

"I'm not certain," Winifred said. She pressed her lips together and leaned over Xavier, who was wallowing on the floor and moaning like a cow. "What is it, Mr. Wormeley?"

"I'm sick, that's what!" he cried. "Can't you see I'm unable to walk?"

As Winifred squatted beside him, Thomas's mind reeled back to a scene he'd witnessed through the very window he stood before now. It was that night after Nicholas's party, when he'd watched Xavier prancing about the ward.

Thomas took a step forward. "Mistress Winifred?"

She looked up at him—and then past him. She stood up abruptly and made for the door. "Someone get this man back into bed," she said. "Sonny, you come with me. We have wounded men coming in."

Thomas whipped around in time to see two soldiers coming in the ballroom door carrying a man who wore more dirt and bandages than clothes. Thomas's stomach turned over.

Wounded men. Wounded soldiers. From the battle.

"Look alive, sonny!" Winifred snapped. "If you aren't going to help, then get out of the way!"

Her words cut through him, and Thomas felt unexpected tears stinging his eyes. He could hardly move for the fear that grabbed at him everywhere.

"Stop gawking and get this man into a bed! And get a basin of water and some towels! Come on, sonny, you're useless standing there!"

"Come on, Hutchinson," Francis said softly at his elbow.

"You'll need some help with that."

With feet of lead, Thomas followed Francis to an empty pallet, glancing over his shoulder only once at Winifred.

I was going to help her, he thought bitterly. *But she can just have Xavier Wormeley yelling at her for all I care. Let her see how it feels.*

Then he smeared the tears away with the back of his hand and turned to Francis. "What do I do, sir?"

That day and the next two stretched out into a long line of things Thomas didn't want to do. He didn't want to see soldiers' dirty faces, lined with rivers of sweat and pain-filled winces. But there were hundreds of them on pallets on the floor of the ballroom, looking up at him, some holding their hands up to him, and a few calling out, "Boy, could I have some water?" But he helped take care of them.

He didn't want to learn to change the dressings on their wounds and see the blood and the torn skin and the way they scrunched up their faces when he pulled away the cloth. But Winifred seemed to be made of iron as she led him from bed to bed and barked at him until he could finally wash the wounds and wrap clean cloth around them by himself. Many of the soldiers told him he was a fine young man.

He didn't want to stand in the doorway with soldier after soldier leaning against his shoulder until a bed could be found, smelling their sweat and their gunpowder and what Thomas was sure must be their pain, too. But he did it every morning when the creaking wagons brought yet more loads of groaning men swathed in bandages with red splotches oozing through. Most of them thanked him and some asked for him when it was time for a bath or a meal. One of them even said he was glad Thomas wasn't out there fighting.

"I'm only 11," Thomas told him.

"You look much older," the soldier told him, patting his arm. "I'm glad you're not."

There were only two things he did want to do. One he did every chance he got.

"Have you seen this soldier?" he would ask the wounded men. And he would hold the miniature of Sam before their pain-strained eyes. Every time, they shook their heads no.

The other thing he wanted to do was talk to Caroline, at least to tell her to be careful about her father because Malcolm wouldn't lie for her again. But every time he tried to speak to her, she bristled like Martha and turned away. Of all the things that were happening, that was the worst.

"We need more salt petre for these wounds, sonny!" Winifred said to him one afternoon. "I sent that little missy for it an hour ago. Has that apothecary gone to the mines for the salt?"

"I don't know."

"We need salt of ammonia or every wound we've dressed is going to fester. And I need some boiled horsehair! That boy's stitches came undone on the wagon. They toss these men around like they're sacks of corn meal!"

Thomas chewed at his lower lip. So what was she asking him to do, he wondered wearily. Stitch someone up? Train the wagon drivers? What?

"So go!" she cried.

"Where?"

"Don't be an idiot, boy! To the apothecary's! I need those supplies now! Salt petre, salt of ammonia—"

"Don't scream at me! You don't have to scream at me!"

The whole ward was suddenly silent, and Thomas took one anguished glance around before he turned on his heel and tore out the door.

I couldn't help it, he cried out to himself as he stumbled down the Duke of Gloucester Street. *I just couldn't help it.*

He was nearly in tears when he got to the apothecary shop, and he choked them back as he opened the side door. But the shop was empty. With a strange kind of quiet that made Thomas look into all of the rooms and call out, "Mr. Pickering? Are you here, sir?"

Thomas heard light footsteps above him, and then a door creaking open in the hall.

"Tom, is that you?" said a timid voice.

"Caroline?"

Thomas ducked into the back hall and saw her standing in the doorway that led to the rooms Francis lived in upstairs.

"What were you doing up there?" he said.

And then he stopped. Her face was as pale as the white bed linens she had clutched against her.

"Mr. Pickering said to warm these, Tom," she said. Her words shook like fragile teacups.

"For who? Who has a fever?"

"For Master Francis, Tom! I'm afraid he's going to die!"

✢ ⋯✢⋯ ✢

Chapter Fifteen

"He was coughing so hard that he could hardly stand up!" Caroline said. "He asked me to help him get upstairs to bed. He said to warm these sheets for him so he could wrap up in them and then he'd be fine. But I don't think so, Tom." Her brown eyes were swimming with tears.

The time that had been grinding on so slowly suddenly began to move ahead like a galloping horse. And Thomas was on it.

"No," he cried. "There's going to be no more dying and no more leaving, do you hear? Now, you warm those linens by the fire and then bring them upstairs."

Caroline's head bobbed. Thomas darted into the shop and rushed behind the counter, where he rummaged through the shelves and grabbed the rattlesnake root and a bottle of ginger syrup. He took the steps two at a time.

In Francis's dark bedroom, he heard the rattling of the old man's breathing before he even saw his balding head on the pillow. Francis looked up at him with feverish eyes.

"What are you doing here, Hutchinson? They need you at the hospital."

Thomas gnawed at his mouth as he opened the ginger syrup. "Sir," he said, "would you please lie back and take this medicine? Then we'll wrap you in some warm linens."

Thomas couldn't explain why he was so sure he was doing the right thing. He didn't seem to have any thoughts at all except, *Give him the cough medicine, give him the rattlesnake root, keep him warm.*

It was nearly dark before Francis's fever was down and Thomas could unwrap him and settle him in for a sleep.

"You go on home now, Hutchinson," Francis said as Thomas stoked his fire. "You'll miss young Donaldson's party."

Thomas's heart turned in his chest. Malcolm's party. He'd forgotten all about it.

"I don't want to see you here when I wake up," Francis mumbled. And then he drifted off to sleep.

It was with heavy feet and an even heavier heart that Thomas trudged down the stairs. He made his way toward home through strong gusts of wind that sent the tails of his brown Holland coat flying. Caroline had long since left to take the medicines to the hospital, and Thomas was as lonely as he was tired pushing through another brewing storm by himself.

I didn't let Francis die, he thought. *But what about Malcolm? After tonight, they could come and take him away. And I don't think I can stop them now.*

He waited for the anger to sizzle up his backbone, but it didn't come. He was too tired.

The house was dark and cold when Thomas got there. Up in his room, there was a tiny fire in the fireplace, and his best suit was spread out on the bed. He plopped down miserably beside it and saw a piece of paper pinned to its embroidered cuff. He lit his candle and peered at the writing.

> *Thomas, where were you? No one was there to take Malcolm to meet Papa, and the surprise was nearly spoiled. But Otis headed him off and we have gone on to the party. Please come quickly.*
> —*Mama*

Thomas groaned out loud. *Caroline and I were supposed to walk Malcolm toward the leathersmith's for Papa to pick him up.* He rolled over on his stomach and buried his face into his hands. *Why didn't Caroline do it? She was so excited.*

Thomas suddenly pushed himself up on his elbows and listened. Everyone had gone to the party, Mama said in her note, but it certainly sounded like someone was in the house, though maybe it was just the wind rattling the window panes.

Thomas crept out into the hall. Just then Winifred's door flew open and she stomped out into the hall.

"If you die, I will never forgive you, Nicholas Quincy!" she cried. "Never! Do you hear?"

She stormed down the hall with her back to Thomas, waving a piece of paper over her head and shouting at no one. Thomas was riveted to the spot as she stomped her feet against the floor and her braid swished across her back like an angry cat's tail. When she got to the end of the hall, she cried, "Couldn't you just be selfish—just this once, Nicholas?"

Thomas stared so hard that he missed the fact that she

was turning around—until she was halfway back down the hall coming toward him and met his eyes with her own, red rimmed and streaming. Winifred deWindt was crying.

"I'm sorry," he said. "I heard someone and I—"

"You heard someone all right!" she said. "Mistress Winifred deWindt, losing her mind right here in your hallway!"

And then she threw her back against the wall and slid down until she was but a pile of skirts and tears on the floor. She put her head on her knees and cried—loudly.

Thomas wasn't sure what to do. But he knew he couldn't just close his door and leave her there. Willing his feet to move, he crossed the hall and sat down stiffly beside her. She handed him the damp piece of paper she'd been waving about.

"Read it," she said.

Thomas smoothed it out on his knee and squinted at it in the dim light of the hall.

My dearest Winnie,

Thomas squirmed a little. He was glad he wasn't reading this out loud.

I have a hospital now. I've set up at the Bunch of Grapes Tavern on the road between Yorktown and Williamsburg. But don't think of coming to pay me a visit, my dearest, because they won't let you past the guards. Things are bad. I am up to my elbows in wounded and dying men, and the cannons are so close that they rock the building while I'm working. I am saving lives, though, Winnie, and I feel God's hand in it. The battle will be short, I know, and I will

soon be back in your arms. Please take care of those
arms. You know what I mean.
   —Nicholas

Thomas felt as if he'd just eavesdropped on a conversation he wasn't supposed to hear, and he felt his cheeks going scarlet.

"He feels God's hand in it, sonny," Winifred said. "So it must be right, eh?"

Her question shot through Thomas like an arrow. "I don't know. I've never felt God's hand."

She cocked her red bird-head at him and swiped at her tears with her chapped hands. "That's why I like you," she said. "Most of the time you're honest, and when you aren't being honest, I know it's because you can't stand the truth. We're a lot alike, you know."

Thomas shook his head. He didn't know.

"You're so scared, you want to punch everyone," she said. "I'm so scared I bark at everyone." She sighed. "You know why I'm so afraid?" she said, poking at the letter from Nicholas with her finger. "I'm in love with a man who would do anything for a sick or hurt person, including practically throw himself in front of a cannonball. And I'm fighting a war against sickness and bullet wounds that's more hopeless than the battle at Yorktown." She gave him a sideways look. "So what's *your* story, sonny?"

"My story?"

"Why are you so angry?"

Thomas looked down at his hands and felt the anger pumping up his backbone—not at her, but because his story was surging to be told. And he wanted to tell her. He didn't know why, but she was sitting there beside him just waiting to listen. And he wanted to tell her.

"I hate the war," he blurted out. "Because . . ."

"Go on," she said.

He did. He told her all about Alexander and Sam and Papa and Nicholas. He even told her what he'd done with Malcolm's papers.

"And now everyone is at Wetherburn's celebrating his birthday in front of the whole town, and the militia is sure to find out and come for him anyway."

He swallowed hard so he wouldn't cry. By now Winifred had stopped weeping and was nodding slowly.

"And now even your friend Caroline is in trouble, eh?" she said.

Thomas looked at her sharply. "Caroline? Why?"

"Oh, of course. You weren't there. I'm afraid it's my fault. I took her on as messenger with no regard for her being a Loyalist. I have a mind like a tunnel sometimes."

"What happened?" Thomas said. He clutched the legs of his breeches with his fingers.

"When she came back from Pickering's with the medicine late this afternoon, she was about to head Malcolm down the road—and a man came storming in with his coat-tails flying out behind him, demanding to know where she was. Malcolm said it was her father."

Thomas sank back on his knees, his heart sinking. "Was Malcolm the one who told that she was working at the hospital?"

"I don't know, but the man was quite angry. He grabbed her by the arm and hauled her away like a prisoner."

"I used to like Mr. Taylor!" Thomas cried fiercely. "But now—"

"Hold on, sonny," Winifred said. "You can hardly blame

the man. He said he received a letter—the second one, in fact, and unsigned, of course—this time saying that his Loyalist daughter was suspected of being a British spy, and if he didn't get her out of the hospital, there would be trouble for the Taylors."

"A spy!" Thomas said. "That's stupid!"

"That's what Malcolm tried to tell him. He stood up for her, Scottie did."

That caught at Thomas. "He did?"

"Well, he tried to. But Mr. Taylor knows these Patriots can be such hotheads that they'll believe anything. He was only protecting his daughter from—"

"It was Mr. Wormeley," Thomas said suddenly. "I'll bet anything those letters came from him."

Winifred grunted. "That poor, sick man who is too ill to write?"

Thomas looked down at his toes. "About Mr. Wormeley. I want to tell you—"

"I've had enough of talking about that sulking sow," Winifred cut in. "There's something else I want to tell you. I'm sorry that I screamed at you in the hospital today. Very sorry. It was my own fear talking, but I have no right to take it out on you. I only do it because you're tough enough to take it. But that's no excuse. After all, we all have our breaking point." She sighed. "Do you accept my apology, sonny?"

"All right," Thomas said slowly, "but only if you'll stop calling me sonny."

"I will," she said. "If you'll stop calling me Major deWindbag."

"That's Malcolm's name for you!"

"Ah, Malcolm." Winifred cut her eyes at him. "What are

you going to do about him?"

Thomas's grin faded. "I don't know. What should I do?"

Winifred put both hands up as if she were surrendering. "Far be it from me to ever tell another person what he or she should do unless it has to do with a wound or a fever. Only God can tell you what to do."

"God?" Thomas said. He shook his head. "I don't think God cares what I do anymore."

"Hmmm," Winifred said.

Thomas watched her as she leaned back against the wall and kept unfolding her paper.

What was it she had said about "Hmmm"?

"It's all right," Thomas said.

"What is?"

"You say 'Hmmm' when you think I don't want to hear what you have to say, but I do."

"All right, then," she said in her crisp way. "I think you still believe God decides everything. But since things aren't going your way, you don't like the way God's doing it and you're afraid that what God has decided isn't what you want."

Thomas felt his face twisting into a question mark.

"Take Sam," she said. "Just because Sam *may* have been killed in the war doesn't mean God doesn't care. It means maybe God has other plans for Sam. And that scares you."

"Sam is coming home," Thomas said stubbornly.

"All right," Winifred said. "Let's consider Malcolm, then. You think God doesn't care because He's allowed the militia to find out about Malcolm. But maybe God has plans for Malcolm that include his going to war. God will take care of him—you don't have to."

"But what about me?" Thomas said.

"God has His hand on you, Thomas Hutchinson," she said. "I can see that. How do you think you knew what to do for Francis this afternoon? If you aren't destined to become a doctor, then I have two heads."

Thomas looked at her quickly, and she gave her husky chuckle. "No, I know I'm not a beautiful woman, but I don't have two heads."

Thomas looked at his hands, his toes, anyplace but at her. "I used to pray a lot," he said finally, "and I used to think God was right beside me." He shrugged sheepishly. "One time I even stuck my hand up in the air to see if God would touch it. Pretty stupid, eh?"

Winifred shook her head and waited.

"But now," Thomas went on, "I don't know. Sometimes I think it's just all up to me."

"All right, then," Winifred said, "you've prayed, but you haven't listened to God's answers because you've gone right on and tried doing it all your way. Try feeling God's hand, and see what happens. Then you decide if God cares."

"That's what Papa said, and Dr. Quincy, but—"

"The noise of your anger was probably too loud then. But try it now."

"How do I *do* that, though?" Thomas said.

"Ask God to help you," she said. "And then wait quietly. You'll feel it."

She patted his shoulder and struggled to her feet. "I have to get back to the hospital," she said. "Are you going to the party?"

Thomas shrugged. She went into her room and came out with a cape, which she swung around her shoulders as she looked at him.

"Malcolm will be glad to have you there, no matter what has happened between you two," she said. "I've seen him looking at you with a sad face sometimes. He misses you. And you miss him, you stubborn mule."

She poked at him playfully with her toe and then swished off down the hall and down the stairs. In a moment, the front door closed, and Thomas was left alone again. The house was silent. He closed his eyes.

"You don't like the way God's doing it," she had said.

Thomas chewed at his lip. It reminded him of somebody else—where had he heard something like that recently? And then he remembered. The story he had read to Louis.

What was that fellow's name? Naaman. He didn't want to dip in the Jordan River. He thought Elisha should come to him himself.

"You don't like the way God's doing it. You're afraid that what God has decided isn't what you want. Ask God to help you."

"Help me, please, God?" he said out loud. "I'll try it Your way, but I don't know what it is."

He listened for God. He heard only the wind, and then a pounding on the front door. It was a pounding he had heard before.

✢ ✢ ✢

Chapter Sixteen

"Good evening, Master Donaldson," the officer said. "I see I haven't caught you in your nightshift this time."

Thomas looked down blankly at his brown Holland coat and breeches and the money pouch still fastened around his waist. When he looked up, the militiaman was holding out a rolled piece of parchment.

"These are your orders, Donaldson," the officer said. "Report as stated."

"Yes, sir," Thomas said faintly.

"All right, then. Good evening." Thomas stood frozen in the doorway until the clicking of the man's heels on the stone walk had long since been swallowed up by the storm.

"You've tried doing it all your way," Winifred had said, "now try feeling God's hand and see what happens."

Slowly, he tucked the parchment into his money pouch and headed for Wetherburn's Tavern.

As he made his way down the Duke of Gloucester Street past the Courthouse, Thomas had to bend his head against the gusts. Leaves were swirling around him in eddies too turbulent for just autumn. This was a live storm with a biting wind that took his breath away.

Thomas turned his collar against it and hugged his arms around him as he plowed through. He had just stepped off the walk to cross the street to Wetherburn's when he heard someone shouting.

He peered through the storm and was almost bowled over by a figure hurling toward him, hair plastered to her face by the wind.

"Tom!" Caroline shouted to him. "Come quick, it's Mr. Pickering!"

She grabbed his hand, and Thomas held on as she pulled him down the Duke of Gloucester Street toward the apothecary, the wind trying to smash them against the shops.

"What's wrong?" Thomas shouted to Caroline as they slid up the slippery steps. He pried the door open against the wind.

"He's worse," Caroline said. She kept talking and gulping for breath as she led him up the stairs.

"I thought you would be locked in your room," Thomas said.

"I was, but I decided to slip out the window and at least check on Mr. Pickering."

They had reached the doorway to Francis's room, and Caroline's brown eyes were wide with fright. "He can hardly talk, Tom. He's burning up and wheezing."

Thomas leaned over the balding, feverish head.

"Sir?" he whispered. "Can you hear me?"

There wasn't even a groan. Just the fearful clacking of his breathing, as if someone were dragging a stick along a picket fence. Thomas's heart leaped up to his throat.

"What do we do, Tom?" Caroline cried.

Thomas tried to hear himself think over the rat-a-tatting. *I don't know!* he wanted to shriek at her. *We're only just a boy and a girl. How are we supposed to know what to do?*

But then above it, he seemed to hear another voice—Winifred's voice saying, *"How do you think you knew what to do for Francis this afternoon?"*

"You stay here and do the same thing we did before," Thomas said to her. "I'm going to go get Winifred. And Caroline, pray," Thomas added as he charged for the door. "Pray really hard."

The storm was raging like an angry bull now as Thomas looked out the window in the apothecary door. He pulled up the collar of his Holland coat.

"Take this, Tom," Caroline said behind him.

She was holding out Francis's old black cape, frayed at the edges from years of scuttling about town in winter, delivering his medicines. She put it around his shoulders, and Thomas clutched it to him. It barely covered his knees, but it smelled of ginger and cinnamon. Somehow it gave him more strength to open the door and plunge out into the blistering wind.

I'll just get to Winnie and she'll know what to do, he told himself over and over as he pushed through the wind.

He kept his face to the ground as he plunged on to keep the wind from stealing his breath. Only when he reached the corner of the Palace Green did he look up—and see the flames dancing from out of the roof of the Palace hospital.

Thomas stopped and gaped—until a new gust knocked him sideways and sent the fire racing across the top of the building.

"Fire!" he screamed as he tore toward the Palace.

A waddling figure clad in purple burst from around the side of the building, screaming, "Fire! Help! Fire!"

Then the front door flew open and smoke billowed out and was snatched up by the wind. From out of the fog, bandaged, limping men stumbled as if they were fumbling their way out of a bad dream.

"Buckets! Buckets for water!" someone cried. "Get all the buckets you can!"

Suddenly, Thomas was surrounded by a tangle of confusion. Patients were dropping to the ground, coughing and hugging their bandaged limbs. Men were shoving past him, leather buckets sloshing water on their hands. Frantic townspeople in shifts and nightcaps were clutching their flapping capes about them and crying, "Are there still people inside?"

"Is Louis in there?" Thomas cried. "Where's Winnie?"

He hurled himself toward the building, only to feel a heavy hand on his shoulder. "You stay here, son, and help with the patients as Malcolm and I bring them out!"

Thomas looked around only once to see the knot of people in bright silks and laces still wiping the crumbs of ginger cakes and plum tarts from their faces as they stared in disbelief at the fire. Malcolm swept past him in his new brick-colored silk and ran after Papa into the burning building.

"Thomas, over here!"

Thomas whipped around and followed Winnie's voice to the middle of the Palace Green.

"Get the patients out of the wind," she shouted. "See if any of their wounds have opened!"

"No, take them to the church!" It was frail Reverend Pendleton, pulling a greatcoat over his nightshift.

"Good, then!" Winifred said. "Thomas, we're going to

need medicine. Does Francis have more?"

Thomas pawed at her arm. "He does. But Mr. Pickering is dying, Winnie!"

For a moment, the fire disappeared behind her, and Winifred searched Thomas's face with her smoke-red eyes. "Then you go to him," she said finally. "We can handle this."

"What do I do?" Thomas cried.

But she was already gone, pulled away by the wind and the terror of the burning building.

"Try feeling God's hand and see what happens," she had said.

"But I don't feel it!" Thomas shouted into the noise around him. "I don't know what to do. I need Nicholas or—"

Nicholas. Nicholas at the Bunch of Grapes Tavern.

Wrapping Francis's cape tightly around him, Thomas tore across the Palace Green, away from the flaming hospital.

"Thomas, where are you going?" he heard his mother call.

"I'm going to take care of Mr. Pickering!"

But he didn't go to the apothecary shop. He ran straight to the Hutchinsons' stable. Burgess was stomping in the corner stall, winnying nervously at the smoke.

"I know it scares you," Thomas said softly to the horse as he hauled a saddle over his back. "But don't worry. I think God is with us."

I hope so anyway, he thought as he buckled the saddle in place with shaking hands. *I hope Winnie was right.*

The Palace Green was crowded as Thomas galloped past and down the Duke of Gloucester Street.

For six miles, they ran without stopping, Thomas bent low over the saddle so the brutal wind wouldn't suck the breath from him. By the time they were halfway to Yorktown, the beginnings of a drizzling rain joined the wind, and even bringing his face close to Burgess's mane didn't keep the spray from stinging his cheeks.

He had to watch carefully where he was going. He would be coming up on the Bunch of Grapes soon—and Nicholas would be there, and it would be all right.

But before the roadside tavern came into view, Thomas saw a soldier, standing in the middle of the road, holding up his hand. Heart plunging, Thomas reined in Burgess.

"Halt, I say!" the soldier cried. He looked up at Thomas with a face shimmering with rain. Thomas bit at his lip.

He'd seen the face before. It was young—younger looking than Malcolm. It was the soldier he'd seen wrapping his blistered foot that day he and Papa had gone to the James River.

But the boy didn't seem to recognize him. He only drew himself up importantly and said, "You can go no farther. There is a battle going on down there, you know."

"I know!" Thomas said. Somewhere in the turmoil of his mind, he thought, *It's as if he's playing a pretend game.*

The young soldier adjusted the rifle he was holding awkwardly across his chest. "I cannot allow you to pass."

"But I have to pass!" Thomas said. "I have to see—"

"Only soldiers are allowed from this point on."

Thomas clung desperately to Burgess's reins. "You don't understand! Please!"

"Look, you can't go, all right?"

The words were spat out the way Thomas himself might have said them in anger. He looked as if there were many things he would rather be doing than standing in the middle of a Virginia storm, up to his ankles in mud—especially with an oozing blister on the bottom of one of his feet. The game wasn't fun anymore.

I know this game, Thomas thought suddenly. *And I can play it better than he can. Caroline even said I played it best.*

"You don't understand," Thomas said again. "I am a soldier."

"Where is your uniform?"

Thomas hugged the cape around him. "I don't want to get it as wet as you are. Please let me pass. I have to see the doctor. I'm . . . I'm his assistant."

A gust threatened the soldier's hat, and he clutched it with one hand and looked up into Thomas's face. "I've been to the doctor. I didn't see you."

"I saw *you,*" Thomas said. "He put salt of ammonia in the blister on your foot to keep it from rotting, right?"

The soldier stared through the rain that dripped from his eyebrows. "That's right." He looked around helplessly, and Thomas's heart began to race with hope. "Even if you are the surgeon's assistant, without official papers, I can't let you pass."

Again, Thomas's heart dove. Papa was always prepared for things like this. That day they'd gone to the James River, he had simply whipped the proper papers out of his money pouch.

"Oh!" Thomas cried suddenly. He fumbled with the buckle on his own money pouch and pulled out the roll of parchment. "These papers?"

The soldier snatched the roll from his hand and peered at them through the rain. His face crumpled with relief. "These are the ones!" he said happily. "You're Malcolm Donaldson, then?"

"Yes," Thomas said. "I'm Malcolm Donaldson."

✠ ⁘ ✠

Chapter Seventeen

"Go, then!" the soldier cried. He shoved the now limp roll of parchment at Thomas and backed gratefully away toward the side of the road, where the shelter of a tree awaited him.

Thomas stuffed the paper back into the pouch. Without bothering to fasten it closed, he dug his heels into Burgess's sides and spurred on through the rain. Icy sheets were starting to pelt down from the sky, but Thomas didn't care now. He tossed the wet tendrils of black hair out of his face and rode with his eyes up, searching for the Bunch of Grapes Tavern.

And two miles later, there it was—a ramshackle building blazing with lanterns and crawling with soldiers carrying large bundles over their shoulders. It was only when Thomas got down from Burgess that he saw that the bundles were actually soldiers, arms dangling, eyes closed, faces bloody.

And it was only then that Thomas realized the roar he was hearing behind it was the deafening sound of cannons and gunfire.

Fear wrapped itself around Thomas's middle like a vice, but he pushed himself past the groaning soldiers and into the tavern. The first person he saw, bent over a high table, was Nicholas.

"This fellow is ready to be taken upstairs," he called out. Thomas jumped at the sound. The quiet Quaker voice seemed to have disappeared. But it came back as he said to the soldier on the table, "I think we've saved that leg, sir."

Nicholas lifted his eyes for his next patient, and his face lit up in the gloom.

"Thomas!" he cried.

Thomas flung himself into Nicholas's arms. It was going to be all right now.

Nicholas held him for a minute, and then pushed him out to arm's length. "Thomas, what are you doing here?"

"Mr. Pickering is dying," Thomas said. He felt his mouth trembling into a grin, full of sweet relief. "He's got a terrible cough and fever. I know you can help."

"Why didn't you ask Winnie?" Nicholas suddenly looked frightened. "Is Winnie ill? Is it her—?"

"There was a fire at the Palace," Thomas cut in. "She was too busy with the patients. But I know *you* can save him."

Nicholas stopped and looked at him sadly. "How can I do that, Thomas? I can't leave here."

He spread his arms out to the room, and Thomas looked around. Every inch of space held a soldier, propped against a wall or slumped in a corner. Every one of them was waiting for Nicholas to save his arm or his leg or his life.

The smile slid off of Thomas's face. "But Mr. Pickering is dying."

"Then you must save him, Thomas. I can tell you what to

do, and you can do it. Now—" He stood up and turned to the shelves on the wall behind him. "We have some new treatments I have learned from the doctors here. It's a cough and fever Francis is plagued with?"

Thomas could only nod. His mind couldn't hold anything except one thought: *Winifred said if I did it God's way, it would be different. But I thought Nicholas would come back with me if I did it God's way. I thought God would care.*

And just because He wants you to dip in the Jordan seven times instead of coming Himself, you think He doesn't care?

Thomas looked up, startled. Had someone said that?

But no one was looking at him, including Nicholas, who was busily writing instructions on a scrap of paper. The thought had come from inside himself.

"Here are the instructions, Thomas," Nicholas said. He turned from the cabinets and held out the paper and a vial of powder. "This tells you exactly what to do with this new medicine."

Thomas stood there, trying to move but frozen with fear.

"Be on your way now, Thomas. And God be with you in the storm."

Thomas nodded, and then flung his arms around Nicholas. The doctor held on. *I want you to come with me,* Thomas wanted to cry. *I can't save Francis alone.* But he peeled himself away and went back out into the rain and hoisted himself up onto Burgess.

"Let's go," he said miserably to the horse. "I have you . . . and I sure hope we have God."

By now the night was a solid wall of rain, moved only by the blasts of wind that pushed it first one way and then the other. Burgess tucked his head down and drove into it, but even the big bay could not hold steady against the onslaught of the storm. He stepped fitfully, slipping and sliding, as he and Thomas painfully and slowly pushed their way through toward Williamsburg.

"Come on, Burgess!" Thomas shouted to him. "We have to get the medicine home to Francis!" He dug his heels in, and the horse tried to run. But the wind was so strong that he found himself sideways. "Come on, Burgess! You can do it!"

When they reached the place where the soldier had stopped them, there was no one in sight, and it was easy to see why. The rain was washing the road away, and a stream had already cut across it and was roaring through like the James itself. Burgess leaped over it and charged on.

"That's the boy!" Thomas cried. He dug his knees in harder. "Come on, then. Faster—please!"

Burgess hardened into a stuttering run. Thomas leaned close to him until they were like one, and he peered out from the side. All he could see ahead were torrents of rain in the driving wind, carrying twigs, leaves, and debris. It was as if the whole world were blowing away.

But Francis was dying. That was all Thomas could think about as he charged on . . . until he peered through the storm and saw a tree go down across the road ahead.

"Whoa, Burgess!" Thomas cried. He pulled back on the reins, and the horse's backside went down. But Thomas felt himself being pulled loose from Burgess's back. He heard himself screaming as he hurtled over the horse's head. And then he heard nothing.

Even when he opened his eyes, Thomas wasn't sure

where he was. Things were swaying in and out of focus, from dream to real and back again. He fought to stay in the real part and tried to sit up. His head spun, and he fell back down.

"Burgess!" he called out.

But there was only the fallen tree and the booming of cannons in the distance. Thomas dug his hands into the mud and got to his elbows. The world reeled, and he was gone from it again.

It seemed a long time before it came back. This time he was moving—being dragged along by his armpits to a place that felt drier. He tried to open his eyes, but something large and warm covered them. Someone's hand. Thomas didn't feel like pushing it away. He just closed his eyes and drifted peacefully out again.

The next time, he came crashing awake with a pain searing through his head. He tried to raise it, but he seemed to be tied to something solid and breathing.

"Take him home, Burgess," someone whispered.

Then Thomas heard a slap and he was moving again, jouncing up and down.

You're on a horse, his gathering thoughts told him. *You're tied to Burgess and he's taking you home because someone told him to.* He didn't ask himself any questions. He just held on and let Burgess carry him back to Williamsburg.

He was fully awake by the time they trotted up to the gate at the Hutchinson house. At first there were only voices around him.

"John, it's Thomas! He's come home!"

"Is he alive, Master Hutchinson?"

"Let me get this rope undone, sir."

When Thomas could lift his head, there were faces all around him, smudged with soot and striped by the sweat that had run through it. Mama's eyes were puffy and red as she searched him for signs of life. Malcolm's were intent on undoing the knots that held his legs in place.

"There!" Malcolm said.

Thomas slid from Burgess's back and into his father's arms.

"Otis, take care of Burgess," Papa said, and then he carried Thomas into the house with a chorus of chatter following him.

"Why was he tied to the horse?"

"Where did he go? He told me he was going to Francis's!"

"Whoever tied him on knew what they were doin'. He could have fallen off and been trampled otherwise."

"Enough," Papa said to them as he set Thomas down on the sitting room sofa. "We must find out how badly he's hurt. Thomas?"

"I'm fine, Papa," Thomas said.

He wasn't sure he was fine at all. But he wanted them all to be quiet, because there was something he needed to say. He couldn't remember what it was yet.

"Esther," Papa said. "Get something to wash his face. Malcolm, get a fire going."

Thomas could feel people leaving the room, and he blinked to keep it in focus.

"Thomas, can you hear me, son?" Papa said very close to his face.

"Yes," Thomas said.

"Did someone hurt you?"

Thomas tried to shake his head, but the whole room shifted painfully. "No," he said. "A tree fell across the road. Burgess hit it, and I was thrown. That's all." He licked his lips.

"I'll get some water," Mama said. She floated away.

"Try to hold on now, son," Papa said. "Try to answer my questions. Are you hurt anywhere?"

Thomas tried to take stock of his body, but everything was aching. "I'll be walking like old Francis tomorrow," he mumbled. And then the world came into focus with a jolt. Thomas's eyes sprang open. "Francis!" he cried.

"Easy, there. Quiet, son."

"But Francis! Mr. Pickering is dying!"

"I know," Papa said softly. "He's at the Taylors'."

"But Papa, I have medicine! Dr. Quincy gave me medicine for him!"

He tried to keep his focus on Papa's face.

"You've had a rough go of it, son," his father said. "A bump on the head like that—"

"In my money pouch!" Thomas pleaded. "Please look in there! There's a little piece of paper!"

Papa sighed and unbuckled the pouch, which was still attached to Thomas's waist. Thomas kept his eyes glued to his father's face as he pulled out the small paper and read. Papa fumbled with the pouch again and pulled out the vial.

"Where did you get this?" his father asked.

"From Dr. Quincy. Papa, you have to get it to Mr. Pickering."

"Nicholas? In Yorktown?"

"At the Bunch of Grapes," Thomas said. "I rode there. Papa, please."

His father nodded and stood up.

"Where are you going, John?" Thomas heard his mother say.

"Thomas can tell you what to do for his head," John Hutchinson said. "I'm going to the Taylors'."

"Dovesdung plaster and tansy seed oil, Mama," Thomas murmured.

Virginia Hutchinson bent over him, eyes beside themselves with worry. "I'll go get them, then," she said.

"Are you all right, lad?" Malcolm said, when she was gone.

"I think so," Thomas said.

"How did you end up tied to the horse? Do you know?"

Thomas crooked his finger at Malcolm, who inched closer. "Don't think I'm foolish or anything, Malcolm," he whispered.

"I won't. Why?"

"I think I *know* who it was. I think it was Sam."

"Sam? Your *brother* Sam?"

But Thomas didn't answer him. His eyes drifted closed, and he was gone again, this time into a deep, sweet sleep.

✢ ✢ ✢

Chapter Eighteen

"**W**inifred was right again," Thomas said. He groaned as he changed positions on his bed to reach for his cup of hot cocoa.

"About what, lad?" Malcolm said.

"She said I'd be moving like Francis Pickering after that fall, and I am."

"Francis Pickering is moving, too—thanks to you."

Thomas tried to find a comfortable way to arrange his legs. "I bet he's moving better than I am. I've been in bed for a whole day, and I still hurt."

"Do you expect a miracle? Mistress Winifred said the blow to your head from falling out of the tree was bad enough, then you put this one on top of it."

"Change the subject," Thomas said. "What does Caroline say about Francis? Is he getting better?"

Malcolm dusted his hands off on the backs of his buckskin breeches and frowned. "I haven't talked to Caroline since the day her father dragged her out of the hospital by the hair."

"By the hair?"

"No, I'm exaggerating. But he was mad enough to—and still is. And since his mill burned down in the storm, and no one would help him, he won't talk to anyone outside the family except your father and Francis. Naturally, he isn't going to let Caroline—"

"His mill burned down!" Thomas said. "What happened?"

"I think you can guess. Remember the last storm when a couple of his sails were damaged?"

"Yes."

"There was talk then that the friction of the brake on the windmill could start a fire if it was used during a strong wind. They say Mr. Taylor was trying to stop the sails during the storm, and that's probably what happened." Malcolm shook his shaggy head. "I thought he knew better than to do that. Anyway, no one would help him, and the whole thing went up in smoke."

"Everyone was at the other fire," Thomas said.

"It wouldn't have made any difference," Malcolm said. "You know how they all hate Robert Taylor for being a Loyalist. I tried to tell you that, lad."

"I want to see Caroline!" Thomas said.

"Well, I see our patient is feeling better. Back to his old self, he is!"

Winifred strode briskly into the room, braid swaying, blue-gray eyes sparkling. Her face was acorn-shiny and as close to a smile as it ever came. She put a ruddy hand on Thomas's forehead. "Giving orders again, are you?"

"You said we were a lot alike," Thomas said.

"That I did," Winnie said. "And it seems I was right. But did you have to take it to such extremes?" She shook her head as she peeled the plaster from Thomas's forehead and peeked under it. "Riding a horse through that storm, getting through the soldiers' blockade—"

"There was a soldiers' blockade?" Malcolm said.

"I'm sure there was," Winifred said crisply. "Nicholas said so in his letter."

Malcolm shot question marks at Thomas, and Thomas squirmed.

"Hold still," Winifred said.

"So how did you manage to get through, lad?"

For the first time since he'd come home, Thomas remembered the papers in his money pouch. He looked up to see Winifred studying his face.

"You know what I think you need now, sonny?" Winifred said suddenly. "I think you need to get out of this bed and go downstairs for a change of scene. See that the couch is ready, would you, Scottie?"

Malcolm left the room, and Winifred helped Thomas sit up.

"You haven't told Malcolm about the militia yet, have you?"

"How did you know?" Thomas asked.

She looked at him at last and lifted her eyebrows. "I can feel it, sonny."

Thomas thought for a moment. "Would you hand me my money pouch, please?"

She did, and Thomas opened it and pulled out Malcolm's orders, the ink now in streaks, the corners curled. "I'll give these to him today," he said.

Winifred nodded and reached for the pouch. But suddenly Thomas dug his hand into it and felt his heart sink.

"What's wrong, sonny?" she said.

"The picture of Sam," he said. "It's gone! It must have fallen out sometime that night. I didn't close the pouch after I got past the guard!"

Thomas blinked hard, and Winifred patted his shoulder.

"I want to see his face again," he said thickly.

"Perhaps you will," she said. "Come on, then. Let's go."

The trip down the stairs was exhausting, and Thomas was glad to be settling in on the sofa, even with Esther, Mama, Winifred, and Malcolm all scurrying around.

Papa chuckled at the scene. "You're getting more attention than Xavier Wormeley."

"Ugh!" Thomas cried. "Let me up!"

"How is the old windbag?" Papa asked, easing himself into a chair.

"Mr. Wormeley can no longer feign illness," Winnie said, "since he was last seen running for his life from the burning building. So much for the man who couldn't get out of bed, eh?" She took a cup of bee balm tea from Esther and handed it to Thomas. "We are already setting up a new facility at the college. In fact, I must be on my way to supervise. Louis does a wonderful job, but sometimes his sign language falls a bit short."

"Louis?" Thomas said. "Louis is—?"

"My assistant. But only until you come back to work, sonny. We are fine partners, you and I."

She nodded at him, and as she turned to leave, he was sure he saw the twitch of a smile at the corners of her lips.

But before she went two steps, there was a pounding from the front door.

"Shall I get that on my way out?" she asked.

"Please," said Mama.

Papa smiled at the door as Winifred closed it behind her. "She's a fine woman, that one," he said.

"Yes, she is, sir," Malcolm said.

Thomas was staring at him when Mama put in, "Just as soon as Nicholas comes back, I want to start planning the wedding."

"What wedding?" Thomas asked. He felt as if his mind were going in 10 different directions . . . until a voice from the doorway said, "Good day, sir!"

Papa stood up, and Thomas followed his gaze. And then his mind stopped completely.

The militia officer stood outlined by the door frame.

All eyes were turned to the man. Thomas put down his tea. Then he slid down as far as he could on the couch and pulled the covers up over his nose.

He's come looking for Malcolm. I can't let him see me. I have to think. I have to . . . I have to do it God's way.

"To what do we owe the honor of your visit?" Papa said.

His voice was tight. Mama hurried to him and took his arm. It was only then that Thomas realized it might not have been Malcolm he had come about at all.

"I'm afraid I have bad news for you, sir," the officer said.

The room went still as a tomb.

"Go on," Papa said stiffly.

"We were expecting your son to report for duty yesterday at the militia camp on the James. He was to go with his company to reinforce the troops at Yorktown today."

"I don't understand," Papa said.

"Neither do we." The officer coughed uneasily. "By mere coincidence, a young soldier acting as guard on the Yorktown Road was sent back to our camp yesterday, and when our captain was asking if anyone had seen the new recruit yet, this soldier said he had. He'd met him when he was on his way to report for duty—at the surgeon's station on the Yorktown Road. This young guard was too inexperienced to realize the boy was going to the wrong place."

"I am completely confused!" Papa said. "My son has been gone for nearly a year."

"Sir, he showed the young guard his papers. They clearly said 'Malcolm Donaldson.'"

"That's *my* name!"

Malcolm's face was already going ashen.

The militiaman stared back at him. "You are not Malcolm Donaldson. I met the young man. He's much bigger than you, with broader shoulders and—"

"So what has happened?" Mama said. "What is your sad news?"

The officer pulled his eyes away from Malcolm. "The boy—whoever he is—is missing," he said. "I think we can only conclude, sir, that he is a deserter or—"

"No!" Malcolm cried. "Malcolm Donaldson is no deserter!"

The room was suddenly abuzz with confused chatter, and Thomas wished Winifred was still there.

"I can't tell you what to do," she would say. "Only God can. Try doing it His way and see what happens."

The hubbub rose to a fever pitch around him.

"I am Malcolm Donaldson, but I am no deserter! I never saw any papers!"

"We have not heard from our son for three months."

"And this is not our son!"

"I don't understand!"

"I do."

They all stared at Thomas in stunned surprise as he pulled the blanket from his face and struggled to sit up.

"*There* is Malcolm Donaldson!" the officer said.

Before the questions could erupt again, Thomas shook his head. "No, sir," he said. The heartbeats in his throat were making it hard to talk, but he rubbed his sweaty palms on the blanket and went on. "I only told you I was Malcolm Donaldson so I could take the papers and hide them."

He looked frantically at Malcolm, who was staring at him in disbelief. "I was on my way to give them to you at the party, but then there was Francis and the fire. I used them to get past the guard. Then I was thrown off the horse, and I didn't remember until just today." He tried to swallow. "I know it was wrong, Malcolm, and I'm sorry and you can hate me again—but I already lost everyone else. I just didn't want you to go!"

And then with all of them watching, he put his hands in front of his face and started to cry. It felt like someone had pulled a rag out of his mouth, and he was free to breathe at last.

"This is indeed serious, Mr. Donaldson," the officer said.

"I am not Mr. Donaldson, sir," Papa said. "My name is John Hutchinson, and I do not think this is as serious as you think."

"But official papers have been tampered with."

"Papers have been tampered with, but not official ones."

Thomas stopped sobbing and peeked out through his fingers, eyes streaming.

"Malcolm Donaldson *here*—" John stopped to put his arm around Malcolm, who was still staring at Thomas "—is my indentured servant. Therefore, he is not required to serve in the militia as are free men."

The officer looked flustered. "I know that indentured servants are not required to serve, but I was not told that he was a servant when I was given his name!"

Papa's eyebrows shot up. "By whom?"

The officer put his hands to his side curls to think. "We received a message from someone at the hospital . . . and then a second message telling us when his birthday was." His eyes grew clear. "I believe it was Xavier Wormeley."

"That bellowin' cow!" Esther burst forth.

"Oh, that he is, Esther," Papa said. "And he shall hear from me."

Thomas's mind flipped back to the day at the hospital when Caroline had innocently told Xavier the date of Malcolm's party. *I'll never tell her what she did,* he decided.

"Perhaps Mr. Wormeley didn't know that young Donaldson here was a servant," the officer said.

But the general grunt in the room clamped his jaws shut again.

"However," Papa said, "I do have the right to allow Malcolm to serve if he chooses."

Thomas jerked his hands away from his face. *Do it God's way, even if it isn't your way,* his thoughts shouted at him. He bit back a "No!" and glued his gaze to his father.

"What do you say, Malcolm?" Papa said. "You are 16 now. I know how much winning this war means to you. The battle at Yorktown is not yet finished. Would you like to go and serve in the militia?"

Thomas closed his eyes and felt the tears burning their way out from under his eyelids. *"I wish I were there. I haven't fired a shot to help."* He had heard Malcolm say those things a hundred times. Only because of Thomas had he not gone already.

But there was silence in the sitting room. Thomas opened his eyes to see Malcolm studying his hands while everyone waited. The room itself seemed to be holding its breath.

"I do want to serve," Malcolm said.

Thomas felt the world stop, and his heart with it.

"I've made no secret that I've been angry because I couldn't go, but that is just it—I *couldn't* go. I have a duty to people here."

"But I'm releasing you from your duty to me," Papa said.

"Beggin' your pardon, sir," Malcolm said, "but it isn't just my duty to you. I have my sister to think of."

"Of course," Papa started to say. "I know how—"

"And my brother."

Papa turned his head to where Malcolm was looking—at Thomas.

"If God had wanted me to serve in the war, I would have, sir," Malcolm said. His words were coming more easily now. "But I felt a hand holdin' me here." He grinned his square smile sheepishly. "But that doesn't mean I always liked it!"

"We seldom do when it comes to God's wishes against ours," Papa said. He squeezed Malcolm's shoulder and looked at the officer. "I think that concludes our business with you, then, sir."

The officer nodded. "It's a pity, though," he said. "This kind of loyalty would make good soldiers—out of both of your boys." He looked at Malcolm, then at Thomas, and then bowed politely and left the room. Thomas sank back onto the couch and waited for an ax to fall.

Whether it would have or not, Thomas never found out. Before anyone could recover, the officer burst back into the room. "If you want to see Xavier Wormeley, sir," he said breathlessly, "he's right outside your house. And he's gathered quite a crowd!"

Everyone followed Papa out the door, leaving Thomas struggling to get to his feet. Malcolm looked over his shoulder and dashed back to grab him.

"I suppose you want to go out and see what all the ruckus is about, eh, lad?" Malcolm said.

Thomas searched his face. "You don't hate me, Malcolm?"

Malcolm pulled Thomas up onto his back. "Except for Patsy," he said, "I never had anyone want me around as much as you do, lad." He moved toward the door. "I might be too old to join in your games anymore, and I might be a mite peeved with you for tryin' to arrange my life for me . . . but then, I'm annoyed with you at least once a week anyway. Brothers are like that, aren't they?"

Thomas nodded.

"Come on," Malcolm said. "Let's go see what we're missing."

"One more thing," Thomas said as Malcolm carried him to the door. "Since when did you start thinking Mistress Winifred was a 'fine woman'?"

"Since she took care of you the day I knocked you out of the tree," Malcolm said.

The thickness in his voice kept Thomas from asking any more questions.

The officer hadn't been lying when he'd said there was a crowd. Half of Williamsburg seemed to be gathered in front of the Hutchinsons' house. As Malcolm sat him down on the front steps, Thomas looked curiously for Xavier. He found him—standing next to a white-faced Winifred deWindt. On the other side of her was Peter Pelham, the jailer.

"You're an idiot, Wormeley!" Papa was shouting.

"Call me what you will, Hutchinson!" Xavier shouted back. "But this time even you can't stop me!"

Thomas tugged at Malcolm's sleeve. "Why is Peter Pelham here?" he hissed. "Is someone being taken to jail?"

"You say the very woman who was running the hospital for the Patriots set fire to it?" Papa said in disgust.

Both Thomas's and Malcolm's eyes sprang open.

"It only looked as if she were running it for the Patriots!" Xavier cried. "But as sure as I'm standing here, she's a spy for the British!"

The crowd gaped at Winifred and gasped as one.

"Balderdash!" Papa spat out. "She's a Quaker, for heaven's sake. She believes only in healing the sick."

"I don't care if she says she's the angel Gabriel. She's in cahoots with that stinking Loyalist, Robert Taylor!"

Papa threw his head back and laughed. A few people tittered nervously with him.

"Laugh all you want, Hutchinson!" Xavier cried. By now his face was crimson down to the folds of his flapping jowls. "But I have proof!"

"What proof?"

"She hired Taylor's daughter to work there! She infiltrated the hospital with a Loyalist!"

"Caroline Taylor is 11 years old," Papa said, still chortling. "She couldn't 'infiltrate' a schoolroom!"

"Well . . . be that . . . be that as it may," Xavier stuttered, "I have other evidence to back my claim."

"And that is?" Papa said as he wiped away the laugh-tears.

"I saw her set the fire myself."

Papa's head jerked up. So did Thomas's.

"Who?" Papa said.

"This woman!" Xavier cried gleefully. He pointed a sausage-shaped finger at Winifred. "I saw her do it with my own two eyes!"

✢ ✢ ✢

Chapter Nineteen

"How could he see anything out of those poke holes?" Malcolm said under his breath.

Thomas didn't answer. He craned his neck to see Winifred, who was just then whipping her braid around to face Xavier Wormeley.

"You saw nothing of the kind," she said briskly. "And I'll thank you to take back that accusation."

"I don't take orders from you, woman!" Xavier said. "But now it's you who will be taking the orders from the jailer— maybe even the executioner."

"Don't be ridiculous!"

"I tell you, Hutchinson—and all of you—I saw her! She sneaked out behind the Palace, right where the fire started. I was watching her from the window! She stacked up a load of logs and set a firebrand to them. Then an hour later, she was pretending to care that the wounded got out alive!"

"I have always known you to be a fool," Papa said angrily, "but I never thought you would stoop to something quite this cruel."

"I saw it! Can any of you prove that I didn't?"

A low murmur went through the crowd. But the noise inside Thomas's head was loud—and clear.

Do it God's way. Listen to what He's telling you.

"I can prove it," Thomas said.

Everyone turned to stare at him.

"You, son?" his father said.

"Yes, sir, if you bring Winifred over here."

"What is this nonsense?" Xavier shouted. "It's that boy again. Don't listen to him!"

But everyone seemed eager to hear, and Winifred hurried up to the steps where Thomas sat.

"Get a log, Malcolm," Thomas said. "Get two."

Without a question, Malcolm hurried away.

"He's stalling!" Xavier cried. "Get on with it!"

"What are we waiting for, Thomas?" Papa said.

But Malcolm returned with an armful of firewood.

"Would you stretch out your arms, Mistress deWindt?" Thomas said.

Eyes wary, Winifred did.

"Give her a log, Malcolm," Thomas said.

"But I can't—" Winifred started to say.

Malcolm deposited one chunk of wood into her outstretched arms. They gave way like new willow branches, and the log thudded to the ground.

"It's a trick!" Xavier scoffed. "She's putting on an act!"

"Shut it, Mr. Wormeley!" Papa said tersely. He turned to Winifred. "May I?"

Winifred nodded, and John Hutchinson took one of her arms in his hands. He pulsed it lightly with his fingers and looked into her eyes with his brow furrowed. "You are not a well woman, Mistress deWindt," he said.

Winnie looked at the ground. "Nicholas says my muscles are diseased. Soon my legs . . ."

The face Papa turned on Xavier was etched with The Look. "It is a wonder this woman can lift a spoon, much less a piece of wood big enough to set fire to the Palace," he said. His booming voice grew dangerously low, and Thomas felt his heart start to race. "You have done some despicable things, Xavier Wormeley," Papa went on. "But this—this is the worst yet."

Papa took a breath, but Thomas knew he was only getting started. "This woman left her home in Pennsylvania to come here where she knew the heat of battle was about to rise. She has worked tirelessly, night and day, to care for the sick and wounded—with no reward except what she feels in her own heart. And now you accuse her of a crime she did not commit—a crime she could well have hanged for. And you do it simply because she saw that you were too much of a coward to go to battle and she wouldn't let you get away with it. I won't let you get away with it either. Not anymore. You have defamed the character of an innocent woman, Mr. Wormeley. That is a punishable crime in Virginia, and charges will be filed before sunset today."

The crowd muttered as he took Winifred by the elbow and started to turn her toward the door. Through the murmuring, another voice cried out.

"Si vous plait, monsieur?"

The throng parted like tall grass as Louis pushed his way politely through and looked up at John Hutchinson.

"Yes?" Papa said.

Louis began to speak frantically in French, tossing his

bushy mane of brown hair, and Thomas saw that his usually kind eyes were blazing.

"What is it, sir?" John Hutchinson said. "I'm sorry, I don't speak French. Does anyone here—?"

Thomas tugged at his father's sleeve. "Papa, I think I can help."

By now the crowd was alive with curious chatter again, and they jostled each other with elbows and nodded toward Louis as he made his way up onto the porch with Thomas.

"Show me what you're trying to say, Louis," Thomas said.

Louis nodded a dozen times and looked around wildly.

"Take a deep breath, Louis," Winifred said in the velvet voice she reserved for her patients. "Slow down."

Louis nodded to her, and then he turned to the crowd. Blowing air from his cheeks, he made big motions with his hands and waved them above his head.

"This is ridiculous!" Xavier cried. "The man is a clown!"

"Fire?" Thomas said. "Are you talking about a fire?"

Louis nodded and pointed toward the blackened and collapsed building at the end of the Green.

"The fire in the Governor's Palace," Thomas said.

Louis pointed to himself and then to his eye.

"I . . . saw . . ." Thomas said slowly.

Louis crouched down and, looking over his shoulders as if he were about to steal a plank from the front porch, made the same fire motions between his knees.

"You saw . . . what? You saw someone sneaking and . . . starting the fire!" Thomas cried.

Louis stood up and nodded solemnly.

"Do you know the person?" Papa asked.

Louis nodded with his eyes ablaze. He raised his arm like

a musket and pointed its barrel—straight at Xavier Wormeley.

"*What?*" the fat man cried. "Is he accusing me?"

"It seems he is," Papa said.

"You can't believe this . . . this *charade!*"

"I do," John Hutchinson said. "I daresay you were responsible in some way for the fire at Robert Taylor's mill as well! He would never have made so grave an error himself."

Xavier waved a sausage finger. "No one cares about Robert Taylor's property!"

But someone shouted, "Take him before the magistrates!"

"No, throw him in the jail!" someone else joined in.

Peter Pelham stepped forward and wrapped his hand around Xavier's thick arm. "I think you'd better come with me, Mr. Wormeley," he said.

Xavier was still howling as the jailer pulled him away.

Papa turned and disappeared into the house. Thomas didn't see what happened to Xavier. His own face was buried in the hug that Winifred pulled him into.

"Thank you, sonny," she whispered. And then she chuckled. "I'm sorry. I should say thank you, *Thomas.*"

"It's all right," Thomas said into the gray of her dress. "I like it when you call me sonny."

She let him go and looked at him. Across her acorn-shiny face, a smile appeared, as quick and as crisp as everything else about her.

Then the smile shimmered off her face and she followed Papa into the house. Thomas was about to hobble inside when he heard a "Psst!" from below. He turned painfully just in time to see Caroline beckoning to him from the gardenia bushes. He tried to move closer, but it was still too hard to walk.

"Tell her to come on in," Mama said behind him. "It will be all right for a minute, Caroline. I'm sure it will."

Caroline looked back and then swung up onto the porch and inside the house. Mama ushered them into the dining room and closed the door behind them. It was only then that Thomas saw Caroline had been crying—a lot.

"I have to tell you something," she said in a wavery voice.

The pinched look on her face was scaring Thomas. There wasn't a dimple in sight.

"Just tell me you aren't mad at me anymore," he said. "That's all I want to hear."

"I never stay mad at you, Tom! You know that!"

"All right, then!" Thomas said. He tried to smile and poke her in the side, but she pulled away.

"Stop it, Tom!" she said. "I have to tell you something."

"What?"

"We're going away."

"Who is?"

"My whole family. We're going to Canada—to live."

Thomas could hardly breathe. "Forever?"

She nodded tearfully.

"But why?"

"The mill is gone," she said. "And Papa says the British are losing the battle at Yorktown. As soon as the Patriots have their independence, we'll be run out of town anyway—"

"Don't listen to Malcolm!"

"Stop it, Tom!" Caroline cried. "It's true! Papa says if we don't leave, they'll take all our things and maybe us, too."

Thomas felt as if he were smothering in guilt. "My father can stop them! I didn't tell him about the last time—that day at the mill—but I'll go to him right now!"

Caroline shook her head. "I don't think it will help, Tom."

"But he's always protected your family before."

"I asked my papa that, but he said it's different now."

Thomas swallowed hard against his thoughts. *I could have stopped this—if I'd just told Papa before about George Fenton and the others. I could have made this not be true.*

"We're leaving as soon as Alexander comes home. Papa says it shouldn't be long now. And you said this summer that he was close by. I mean, you didn't say it, but I guessed—"

He's close by, but he isn't with the British, Caroline! Thomas's mind cried out. But he couldn't say, *Don't wait for him. He's a Patriot.* The words wouldn't come. Maybe, he thought sadly, it was God who was holding them back.

"Say something, Tom," Caroline said. Her face was streaming.

"I don't want you to go," Thomas said. The lump in his throat clogged up his words. "I won't be able to stand it."

She nodded and sobbed, and Thomas chewed on his mouth.

It was true. He'd said it about Sam, Alexander, Nicholas, and Malcolm—but it was really true about Caroline. She was the one he wanted to stay most of all.

"I have to go home," she said. "But I won't go to Canada without saying good-bye. They can't make me do that."

Before Thomas could answer, she ran for the door and was gone. Thomas put his head on his arms on the table, and he cried.

It seemed like a long time later that Thomas heard the church bells ringing, and after that he felt strong hands squeeze his shoulders. He smelled licorice and sweat and a little lavender.

"Can I help you, son?" Papa said.

Thomas shook his head. He was limp from crying, and he could barely sit up to look at his father.

"You've had some bad news, eh?" Papa said. He pulled a side chair close and sat down. "I heard about the Taylors. I'm sorry, Thomas. I know how much Caroline means to you."

Thomas chewed on his lip. "I could have stopped it, Papa. But I was so mad at Robert Taylor. And then I got so mad at you—"

"What are you talking about, Thomas?"

"I was there the day the Taylors' mill was first damaged," Thomas said, looking miserably into his hands. "George Fenton and the leathersmith—they were yelling terrible threats at Caroline's father. I should have told you so you could have stopped them. Then the mill wouldn't have burned—and they wouldn't be making Caroline leave now!"

Slowly, Papa shook his head. "It wouldn't have done any good, son. I did all I could for the Taylors and the other Loyalists, but the war has taken that out of my hands now." Papa put his hand on Thomas's shoulder. "The battle at Yorktown is over. The Patriots have won."

Thomas sat up straight. "They've won the battle?"

"Not only the battle—the war. The British have surrendered. We are an independent country."

Thomas stared at him.

"Did you hear the church bells ringing?"

"Yes, sir."

"They were tolling for America."

For reasons he couldn't begin to sort out, Thomas

started to cry again. His father pulled him to his big chest.

"I must tell you something, Thomas. When that officer came to our house today, I thought he was here to tell us that Samuel had been killed. Did you think that, too?"

"I did for a minute, Papa. But I didn't believe it. I've never believed it."

His father nodded slowly. "I set great store by that, Thomas. I haven't allowed myself to believe he was alive, because I am so afraid of being disappointed. But I won't give up hope if you haven't. Not yet."

It was so quiet that Thomas couldn't sleep that night. The sky over Yorktown was silent now. His mind was, too, as he lay in his bed. The noise of the past few weeks wasn't roaring in his thoughts anymore.

But his chest was aching. He turned to his side and sighed from somewhere deep inside himself. A broken heart hurt. And no medicine from Francis or Nicholas or Winifred could mend it. Caroline was going away, and it hurt.

He was still far away from sleep when he heard hoofbeats on the road. They clopped in the mud and then stopped, just in front of the Hutchinsons' house.

Thomas pushed his covers back and crept stiffly to the window. When he pulled back the curtain and looked down into the street, he caught his breath. There in the moonlight was a horse, an unfamiliar one with a plain saddle and only a knapsack hanging from its side. The man who hurried up the walk had his head bent low, and he was wearing a cape.

Thomas rocked back on his knees and hugged his arms around him.

No! Please! he said to God. *Please. I know I have to do it*

Your way, but please don't let him be coming to tell us about Sam. Please—please no.

He stayed there and waited for the pounding on the door, but it didn't come. Thomas was sure he heard the sounds of the outdoors for a moment, as if the door had been opened and then closed. He held his breath and strained forward, and there it was—the creaking of a floorboard. And then a few seconds later, another one.

Someone was sneaking up the stairs. Thomas clapped his hand over his mouth to keep himself from screaming, and his mind clawed frantically for what to do. But before he could do *anything,* he saw his door slowly open and the doorway fill with broad shoulders. Thomas stood up and stared. His voice came out in a whisper.

"Sam? Sam . . . is that you?"

The moonlight glowed on the man's square jaw as he took a step forward. Thomas was in his arms before he could take another.

"Sam!" he cried. "I knew you were alive! I *knew* you were!"

His brother held him tight and breathed a sigh that seemed to come from his toes. "I didn't know if *you* were, though," he said. "The last time I saw you, you were on the back of Burgess, headed for Williamsburg. I couldn't very well tie you on and never come back to see if you made it, now could I?"

"Samuel?" said in a deep voice behind them. "Is that . . . is that Samuel?"

Sam turned, and Thomas felt as if lightning were striking back and forth between the two men.

Papa took the room in one stride and enfolded Sam in

his arms. "Thank God you're still alive," Papa murmured, and Thomas felt his throat tighten. His father was crying.

The next hour was a blur as Mama hurried into the room in her dressing gown and screamed. Esther, Otis, and Malcolm were awakened and a fire was built in the sitting room and food and cocoa appeared from nowhere. No one could stop hugging or asking questions or simply gazing at Sam. When Winifred stumbled in sleepily, there were introductions to be made and more cocoa to be passed—and then more gazing at Sam.

"They act as if he just rose from the dead," Thomas whispered to Winifred.

"I think you're the only one who doesn't think he did," she whispered back.

After Mama had gone over Sam with both hands to be sure he had no broken bones and Esther had plied him with everything from licorice drops to sugar muffins, Sam finally put up his hands and said, "Enough, my beloved family! I am only here until noon and then I must return for the surrender ceremony. We have so little time. Why don't I answer all of your questions, eh?"

Everyone seemed suddenly to cling to each other as they listened. Thomas hugged his arms around himself as he sat at Sam's feet.

"First of all, the reason you couldn't find me with any of the companies, Papa, is that I never actually joined the army. I had to tell you I did in my letters because I didn't know into whose hands those letters might fall before they got to you, and I had to keep my job a secret."

"Then where have you been?" Papa said sharply.

"I have been working with Alexander Taylor."

"As a spy?" Papa said. "But how could that be?"

"Not as a spy exactly. Do you remember how I always talked about Francis Marion and his band of swamp guerrillas who sabotaged the British in Carolina, not in battle but in small, secret attacks in the places they were familiar with—the swamps and the rivers. Do you remember?"

"Of course," Papa said. "You were enthralled with stories of the Swamp Fox."

Sam grinned. "I still am! Alexander and I and some others formed our own band of Swamp Foxes. And who better to do it? I grew up on the plantation, and Alexander grew up here and in Norfolk. There were others from Charlottesville and the like. Among us we know Virginia like a sister. And we've been able to give men like Benedict Arnold and Cornwallis a run for their money. We made sure your boats got down the James—"

"Then it *was* you I saw at Jamestown!" Thomas cried.

"You nearly gave me away, little brother," Sam said, ruffling Thomas's hair. "Though with sharp eyes like that, we could have used you a time or two."

Papa was still gazing at Sam.

"I'm sorry I had to deceive you, Father," Sam said. "But we've been an important part of Lafayette's plan to drive the British into Yorktown, where Washington and his troops could corner them."

"And they've done it," Papa said softly.

"By all rights, we have won the war."

"Then why must you go back?" his mother said.

"There is still work to be done in Carolina and a few other places, Mama," Sam said. He took her tiny hands into his big ones. "But I'll be back to stay very soon. I promise. I only came now to check on Thomas, and to deliver some bad news."

"First, Sam," Papa said, "I do forgive you—make no mistake about that." Thomas was sure his father's eyes were misty again. "I will want to hear every detail of your adventures in due time. But your greatest triumph was finding Thomas, and I cannot thank you enough—"

"It was the strangest thing," Sam said. "I was about to get past a very confused-looking little guard, as I had done with guards a thousand times before, when he gazed at me and then dug into his coat and brought this out." Sam reached into his own jacket now and produced a small oval.

"That's my picture of you!" Thomas cried.

"A little the worse for wear," Sam said, grinning. "The guard said the 'surgeon's assistant' must have dropped it, and he recognized the face as mine." Sam shook his head. "I knew something was amiss so I went to the makeshift hospital, and there you were. I tried to follow you when you came out, but it was difficult, what with the storm. I lost you once—and then there was Burgess." Sam smiled his biggest smile yet. "He was wandering in the woods just a few miles from here. He led me to Thomas."

Thomas stirred uneasily on the floor at Sam's feet. "So the bad news is that you have to go back for a while?"

The smile faded from Sam's face, and he shook his handsome blond head. "I'm afraid that isn't it, Thomas."

Thomas suddenly wanted to cover his ears so he wouldn't have to hear what Sam said next. But closing his eyes, turning his head, plugging his ears—he knew now that didn't keep anything from being just what it was.

Sam put his hand on Thomas's shoulder. "I know this is

going to hurt you most of all, little brother. Alexander Taylor has been killed."

There wasn't a sound in the room—even from Thomas. There were no cries, no questions, no shouting at God. There wasn't even any noise in his head. There was only the deep, deep pain in his heart.

Thomas wasn't sure exactly what happened for the next few hours, except that he sat with his arms wrapped around himself and just hurt. Esther tried to give him tea. Mama hugged him for a while. Sam whispered, "He died doing something he believed in, Thomas. Something he felt God led him to." And they all prayed together for Alexander and his family. Thomas still stayed curled up in his ball. Only one thought crept in. *Do it God's way*, it said.

"I have to take this news to the Taylors," Sam said when their prayers were finished. "Will you go with me, Father? I don't want them to hear it from strangers."

Suddenly, Thomas's head came up. "Don't tell them he was a spy for the Patriots."

Sam's brows scrunched. "But Thomas, how else will I explain—?"

"I don't know," Thomas said stubbornly. "I just don't think they have to know. What difference does it make now?"

There was a stunned silence.

"You feel strongly about this, Thomas?" Papa said quietly.

Thomas nodded as he fought back his tears. "I do," he said thickly. And then he realized something else. "I do, Papa, because I feel God's hand in it."

And then he felt a human hand—Winifred's—squeezing his shoulder.

At dawn, Papa went to the stable for Judge, and Thomas caught Sam at the back door.

"When you go to the Taylors," he said, "will you tell Caroline I'll be waiting at the Chinese Bridge—what's left of it."

Sam grinned. "Are you still making eyes at her, little brother?" he said.

Thomas curled his lip. "No! I'm not making eyes at her. That's disgusting! That's for Nicholas and Winifred!"

"Oh, those are truly disgusting people from what I can see," Sam said. His shoulders were shaking with silent laughter.

Thomas felt his cheeks burning. "That's fine for them. Mama says they're getting married. But Caroline is just . . . just . . ."

Sam ruffled Thomas's hair with his big hand. "You don't have to explain it to me. Caroline is just—" Sam put his fist against his chest "—she's just here. Nothing disgusting about that."

He gave Thomas's hair another ruffle and went out the back door.

The morning mist had already disappeared from over the charred bridge when Thomas finally heard her footsteps racing across the gardens.

She stopped at the end of the bridge to set her basket down and said, "Alexander—"

"I already know," Thomas said.

She ran to him then and plowed into his chest and cried and cried. Thomas didn't care that she smelled like lilacs. He just wanted the pain in her chest to go away. He wasn't sure it ever would.

"We're leaving today," she said into the front of his shirt. "We're leaving almost everything behind and going away."

A sob rattled through Thomas, and he grabbed on tighter to hold it back.

"Why?" she said. "Why does everything have to be so terrible? My brother is gone . . . my home . . . you!"

Thomas waited for the thoughts to start scrambling around in his head, but they didn't. There was only one thought.

"I guess God has other plans," he said.

Caroline pulled away from him. "But what about our plans, Tom? We always had so many, right here on this bridge!"

Thomas shrugged and looked at his shoes in a blur.

"Well, I hate it," Caroline said.

"I do, too," Thomas said.

"You have to promise me two things, Tom Hutchinson," she said fiercely.

"What?" Thomas tried to say.

She went to the end of the bridge and picked up the basket. It growled. "I want you to take care of Martha," she said. "Mama and Papa say we can't take her."

"She hates me," Thomas said.

"She doesn't, Tom. I told her she can't. She knows."

Thomas nodded numbly, and Caroline set down the basket. "And one more thing," she said. "One more thing you have to promise me."

Thomas just looked at her.

"Promise me that you will never, ever, ever forget me the whole rest of your life."

Thomas shook his head as hard as it would shake. "I never will—ever," he said.

She ran to him and threw her ruffled arms around his neck, and then just as quickly she ran away. As he watched her disappear past the blackened ruins of the Palace, Thomas knew he would never see her again.

It was a long, slow walk back to the Hutchinsons' house. Papa met him on the Green and they walked together toward the Duke of Gloucester Street, Thomas carrying the cat-heavy basket.

Papa didn't ask about Caroline. He only said, "There is still much to look forward to, Thomas. You'll finish your growing up with Malcolm and Patsy and watch them go free. Now that Francis is well again, you can go back to work for him. Nicholas will come home soon—and Sam and Clayton. And you've only just begun your friendship with Winifred."

Thomas nodded and tried not to cry again.

When they reached the end of the Green, the bells in Bruton Parish Church were ringing joyfully and people were rushing back and forth across the Market Square in their best clothes, ready to go to the surrender ceremony. Papa watched them for a moment before he spoke.

"I feel no need to go to Yorktown today," he said. "For me, the war has been fought right here." He put his hand to his chest. "Right inside ourselves."

Thomas felt his brow puckering. "I don't understand."

"You have fought your own battles during this war, Thomas," Papa said. "Right there in your own soul. I think you've come through it all feeling God's hand."

I have felt God's hand, Thomas thought as he looked out

over the Duke of Gloucester Street. *Just like Winifred said I would.* He swallowed hard. *I suppose God will take care of Caroline—if I ask Him to.*

Papa touched Thomas's shoulder. "I am proud to say, son, that you've joined God's side, and you're winning that war inside yourself. Do you know what that makes you, Thomas?"

Thomas shook his head and looked where his father was pointing. On the roof of the Courthouse, the new flag flapped proudly in the wind, brilliantly red, white, and blue against the October sky.

"It makes you free, son," Papa said. "No matter what you may have to suffer, you will always be free."

And although there was still an ache in his chest, Thomas straightened his big Hutchinson shoulders and stood tall.

And he was sure he felt God's hand on him.

✢ ⚜ ✢